The April 3rd Incident

The April 3rd Incident

STORIES

Yu Hua

TRANSLATED FROM THE CHINESE BY ALLAN H. BARR

Pantheon Books  NEW YORK

Translation copyright © 2018 by Allan H. Barr

All rights reserved. Published in the United States by Pantheon Books, a division of Penguin Random House LLC, New York, and distributed in Canada by Random House of Canada, a division of Penguin Random House Canada Limited, Toronto.

Pantheon Books and colophon are registered trademarks of Penguin Random House LLC.

The stories in the book were originally published in Chinese in the following publications: "As the North Wind Howled" in *Beijing wenxue* (1987, no. 5); "The April 3rd Incident" in *Shouhuo* (1987, no. 5); "Death Chronicle" in *Shanghai wenxue* (1988, no. 11); "In Memory of Miss Willow Yang" in *Zhongshan* (1989, no. 4); "Love Story" in *Zuojia* (1989, no. 7); "A History of Two People" in *Hebei wenxue* (1989, no. 10); and "Summer Typhoon" in *Zhongshan* (1991, no. 4).

Library of Congress Cataloging-in-Publication Data
Names: Yu, Hua, [date], author. Barr, Allan Hepburn, translator.
Title: The April 3rd incident : stories / Yu Hua ; translation by Allan H. Barr.
Description: First edition. New York : Pantheon Books, 2018.
Identifiers: LCCN 2018011375. ISBN 9781524747060 (hardcover : alk. paper).
ISBN 9781524747077 (ebook).
Subjects: LCSH: Yu, Hua, [date]—Translations into English.
Short stories, Chinese—20th century.
Classification: LCC PL2928.H78 A2 2018 | DDC 895.13/52—dc23 |
LC record available at lccn.loc.gov/2018011375

www.pantheonbooks.com

Jacket design by Tyler Comrie

Printed in the United States of America
First Edition
2 4 6 8 9 7 5 3 1

Contents

Translator's Note

This volume brings together seven stories published in China between 1987 and 1991, during the opening phase of Yu Hua's career. To readers whose first encounters with Yu Hua's fiction have been through later works that adopt a more familiar storytelling manner, these early pieces may seem a little disorienting, but in their own way they reflect the same interest in testing the boundaries of contemporary Chinese literature that we find in *Brothers,* Yu Hua's ambitious novel of 2005–2006.

In the initial stage of post-Mao liberalization in China in the late 1970s and early 1980s, Chinese writers devoted their energies to broaching topics that had been off-limits during the Mao era and broadening subject matter beyond the few themes permitted or prescribed during the era of radical politics. Literary form, however, remained largely conventional and predictable. It was this conservatism of form that Yu Hua and a number of other young authors set out to challenge in the years leading up to the student-led protests of 1989.

Then in his late twenties, Yu Hua was inspired by both the modernist fiction of such authors as Kafka, Faulkner, and Borges and the theoretical writings of Alain Robbe-Grillet, champion of the French New Novel. Like Robbe-Grillet, Yu Hua sought to break with the tradition of classical realism in favor of a new narrative mode that defied commonsense conceptions of order and logic, avoided definitive judgments, and prioritized the subjectivity of his protagonists. In keeping with these aims, Yu Hua's language at this time is often elliptical, indeterminate, and oblique, suggesting multiple possibilities and inviting a range of interpretations. The stories experiment with a variety of narrative strategies, here alternating between first- and third-person narrative, there blurring the line between author and narrator or between real life and nightmare. "In Memory of Miss Willow Yang" traps the reader in a labyrinth of temporal fractures, repetitions, and inconsistencies.

Given the focus in this collection on the individual psyche rather than society at large, politics is generally kept at a distance. Although the "April Third Incident" in the title story might sound like the name of a watershed episode in modern China such as the May Fourth Incident of 1919 or the April Fifth Incident of 1976, Yu Hua's narrative actually has nothing to do with any major historical event, probing instead the acute sensitivity of its anonymous hero.

This is not to say that these stories are detached from contemporary Chinese affairs. "Summer Typhoon," for example, is clearly rooted in the author's observations of life in his hometown in 1976, following the huge earthquake that leveled the northern city of Tangshan that July. Fearing another such tremor, people throughout much of China abandoned their homes and moved into makeshift shelters in any available open space; in the absence of reliable news, rumor held sway week after week. But while vividly evoking the anxiety and uncertainty of that last summer before the death of Mao, this story too is ultimately less a documentary account than an exploration of adolescent longing and inner worlds.

I would like to thank Yu Hua for patiently responding to my queries. I also thank my wife, Peng Xiaohua, for her advice and support.

The April 3rd Incident

As the North Wind Howled

Sunlight had sneaked in through the window and was creeping toward the chair where my pants dangled. I was lying bare-chested in bed, rubbing away some gunk from the corner of my right eye. It must have collected while I was sleeping, and to just let it stay there seemed inappropriate. At the same time I felt there was no need to be rough, and thus I was prying it out rather delicately. In the meanwhile my left eye was idle, so I gave it the job of looking at my pants. I had taken them off when getting ready for bed the night before, and now I regretted tossing them so casually over the chair, where they lay crumpled beside my jacket. As my left eye inspected them, I began to wonder whether while sleeping I had shed, snake-fashion, a layer of skin, for that's just what my jacket and pants looked like. At this point a skein of sunshine reached my pant leg; the little splotch of leaping light made me think of a golden flea. And so I felt itchy all over and had my idle left hand make itself useful by scratching, but there was so much work for it to do that I had to bring in my right hand to help out.

Someone was knocking on the door.

At first I thought the person was knocking on the neighbor's door, but the noise was obviously intended for my ears. I was thrown for a loop. Who would come knocking on my door? I was the only person with a reason to come here, and I was already in bed. Someone must have come to the wrong place. So I decided to ignore the knocking and continue with my scratching. I thought about how whenever I came back after being away I would always give the door a good knock, and get my key out only when I was sure nobody was coming to open it. Now the door was making a colossal noise, as though it was about to cave in. The person outside, I realized, had to be knocking not with his hand but with his foot, and before I had time to think of a response the door fell to the floor with such a crash that it sent shock waves through me.

A brawny fellow with whiskers on his face charged over to my bed. "Your friend's dying, and you're still not up?" he yelled.

I'd never seen this man before and had no idea where he'd come from. "Have you come to the wrong address?" I asked.

"No chance of that," he answered.

His blithe self-assurance made me wonder whether I had somehow gone to sleep in the wrong bed. I jumped up and ran out into the corridor to check the number on the door. But of course the door was now lying on the floor of my apartment. So I dashed back in again and looked for the number on the fallen door. On it was written: 26 Hongqiao New Village, Apt. 3.

"Is this the door you just kicked down?" I asked.

"Yes, it is," he said.

So this *was* my apartment. "You have definitely come to the wrong place," I told him.

Now it was my confident manner that confused him. He stared at me for a moment. "Are you or are you not Yu Hua?"

"Yes, I am," I said, "but I don't know you."

He gave a roar of rage. "Your friend's dying!"

"But I don't have any friends!" I was roaring too.

"That's nonsense, you little philistine!" He glared at me.

"I'm no philistine," I said. "You can see the proof of that in the books that fill my room. If you're trying to off-load this guy on me, I absolutely refuse, because I have never had a single friend. However . . ." I softened my tone. "However, feel free to donate him to my neighbor in apartment four. He's got a lot of pals and I don't think he'll mind if you toss in another."

"But he is your friend, don't try to deny it." He inched closer, as though he wanted to gobble me up.

"Who is this friend you're talking about, anyway?"

He said a name I had never heard in my life.

"That name means nothing to me!" I shouted.

"You fickle little philistine!" He stretched out an arm as thick as my calf and tried to pull my hair.

I shrank back to the corner of the bed, shouting desperately, "I'm not a philistine—and I've got the books to prove it. If you call me a philistine one more time, I'll have to ask you to leave."

He reached across and with his firm, cold hand grabbed my feeble, warm foot. Then he hauled me out of bed and dumped me on the floor. "Hurry up and get dressed," he said. "Otherwise I'll drag you all the way there just as you are."

I knew it was pointless to argue any further with this guy, because he was at least five times stronger than I. He could throw me out the window with as little effort as he would toss out a pair of pants. "Since a dying man wants to see me," I told him, "of course I'm happy to go." I hauled myself up off the floor and began to get dressed.

So that's how, on this lousy morning, a muscleman kicked

down my door and lumbered me with a friend I had no interest in having—and a friend who was about to die, on top of that. What's more, the north wind was howling like a banshee outside. I had no overcoat or scarf, no gloves or hat—all I was wearing was a thin jacket as I went off with the big fellow dressed in full winter gear, to visit this friend I knew absolutely nothing about.

Once we were in the street, the north wind blew me and the big fellow to the friend's house just as quickly as it would blow a couple of leaves off a tree. The doorway was piled high with wreaths. The big fellow turned to me and said dolefully, "Your friend is dead."

Before I had time to consider whether this was a cause for rejoicing or an occasion for grief, I heard a loud chorus of weeping, toward which the big fellow proceeded to push me.

A crowd of tearful men and women surrounded me. "Don't take things so hard," they said to me solicitously.

All I could do was nod and put on a show of being sad, because now there was no point in saying the things I really wanted to say. I gently patted them on the shoulder and patted their hair, showing my appreciation for their condolences. I also shook hands forcefully and at length with several burly men, at the same time promising not to take it so hard.

Then an old lady tottered forward and grabbed my hand as tears poured down her face. "My son is dead," she sobbed.

"I know," I said. "I am very sad, because it all happened so suddenly." I even thought of telling her that her son and I had watched the sunset together just the day before.

My comment had the effect of opening the floodgates still further, and her wails were now so piercing my hair stood on end.

"Please don't take it so hard," I said.

Her crying seemed to subside a little and she began to dry her tears with my hand. Then she raised her head and said, "You need to take it in stride too."

I nodded reassuringly. "Oh, I will do that. But you must take care of your health."

Again she mopped her face with my hand, as though it were a handkerchief. Her muddy, scalding tears made an awful mess, and I would have grabbed my hand back at once had she not been clutching it so tightly. "You need to mind your health too," she said.

"I will mind my health—we all must do that," I said. "We must transform grief into strength."

She nodded. "My son closed his eyes before you could get here—you don't blame him, do you?"

"No, I'd never do that," I said.

Once more she burst out sobbing. After a while she recovered enough to say, "He was the only son I had, but he's dead. You're my son now."

Tugging desperately, I was finally able to retrieve my hand, on the pretext that I needed it to wipe away my own tears—though my eyes were completely dry. Then I said, "Actually, I've thought of you as my mother for a long time now." I had no choice but to say that.

These words provoked her to an even greater cascade of tears. There was not much else I could do but pat her gently on the shoulder, and by the time she finally turned off the waterworks my hand was aching. She took it in hers and led me to another room, saying, "Go in and keep my son company for a bit."

I pushed open the door and went inside. The room was

empty apart from a dead man lying on a bed and covered with a white shroud. The chair next to the bed seemed to be meant for me, so I sat down.

I sat there for a good long time before lifting the shroud to see what the man looked like. I glimpsed a pale face that gave little indication of age, a face I had never seen before. I put the shroud back and thought, So that's my friend.

There I sat, next to the corpse whose face I had just seen but then instantly forgotten. It wasn't my idea to come here—I came simply because I couldn't think of a way to get out of it. Although the man's death had delivered me from a friendship I refused to recognize, this had not relieved me of my burden, for his mother had simply taken his place: an old woman whom I did not know and had no feelings for had become my mother. However distasteful it was that she treated my hand as her handkerchief, I had no choice but to let her dry her tears with it. And in the future, whenever she needed it, I'd have to offer it to her respectfully, without voicing the slightest complaint. It was only too clear what I had to do next. I'd have to fork out twenty yuan to buy a big wreath, I'd have to don sackcloth and wear mourning and guard his coffin, I'd have to weep and wail for ages, and I'd have to parade through the streets with one arm around the cremation urn and the other propping up his mother. And after all that was over, I'd have to sweep his grave every April, not to mention carry on his unfinished labors and perform the duties of a filial son. But the first order of business—and the most important thing as far as I was concerned—was to find a carpenter and get him to rehang the door that the big fellow had kicked down. Right now, however, all I could do was stay with this confounded corpse.

The April 3rd Incident

1

Standing by the window at eight in the morning, he looked out and seemed to see a lot of things, but none of them really registered—he was conscious only of a bright yellow patch on the ground. That's sunshine, he thought. Then, putting his hand in his pocket, he felt a cold, metallic sensation. This rather startled him, and his fingers began to tremble, surprising him all the more. But when his fingers slowly advanced along the side of the metal, the strange sensation did not develop further; it became fixed. So his hand, too, ceased all movement. Gradually the metal lost its chill—it grew warm, as warm as lips. But before long the warmth dissipated. The object seemed to have merged with his fingers, and so it was as though it no longer existed. Its impressive little show was already a thing of the past.

It was a key, its color much like that of the sunlight outside. Its irregular, bumpy teeth somehow conjured the image of a potholed, arduous road, a road that he might one day have to take.

Now he needed to think: To whom was the key related? It would unlock the door. When the key turned in the lock, what would happen? If one imagined a paper fan unfurling halfway like an accordion, that would resemble the arc of the door as it opened—an elegant and unhurried arc, no doubt. At the same time it would make a sound like an accordion's first, fluttering note. If one proceeded to anticipate what would happen next, surely it would be him entering the room from outside. And he would smell a sweaty odor, an odor that was his. At least he hoped it was his, and not his parents'.

As he was imagining himself pushing the door and stepping inside, his body had actually done quite the opposite: to put it simply, he had exited the room and now was standing outside. He stretched out an arm and pulled the door shut. At the final moment he tugged sharply and the door banged against the frame. The noise was so blunt and powerful, it made him— go out.

Without question, he was now walking in the street. But he didn't have the sensation of walking—it was rather as though he were still inside the house, next to the window. In other words, he only *knew* and did not *feel* that he was walking along the street. This realization took him aback.

At that moment a mop of dark hair glided into view. Bai Xue was approaching. For Bai Xue to appear so suddenly and without preconditions came as rather a shock.

She once had sat, dressed in a pale yellow blouse, at a desk diagonally opposite his. The sight of her had touched him deeply then, although he wasn't sure if it was she or her blouse that was responsible. One way or the other, he was to suffer the consequences of his susceptibility to her looks, for later he would get the jitters every time he saw her.

This time, however, when she dropped in front of him like a leaf from a tree, he was only a little flustered.

They had been classmates in the past, but now they were no longer connected in any way. She had stopped wearing that unsettling yellow blouse. But now she was standing in front of him.

She clearly had no intention of moving to one side and letting him pass, so it was up to him to make way. As he stepped down onto the pedestrian crossing, he suddenly realized that he was treading on her pitch-black shadow. To his astonishment, he found that the shadow was stationary. So he raised his eyes and shot her a glance.

She happened to look at him at precisely the same moment. Her glance was most unusual. It was as though she was under great stress. And it was as if she was signaling to him, signaling that there was a trap nearby. Then she hurried away.

He was confused, and only when she had gone some distance did he take stock of his surroundings. Not far away a middle-aged man was leaning against a plane tree, watching him. The man quickly turned his head and looked in another direction, at the same time putting his right hand inside his jacket—into a chest pocket, surely. Then the man's hand came out again, this time with a cigarette between his fingers. The man lit it casually and began to smoke. But he felt the nonchalance was just an act.

2

Though safely ensconced in bed, he hardly closed his eyes the whole night. Outside, all was still and silent beneath a pale moon. Shadows of trees were faintly visible through the curtains.

He was remembering the past. For him to be so sentimental came as a surprise, even to him.

He saw a boy leaving him and going away. In the background was a pond ringed with willow trees. Trotting down a path as long and slender as a rope, every so often the boy would turn around and look back. But the boy showed no reluctance to leave, and he felt no regret at the boy's departure, either. The boy seemed foreign to him, but that graceful face and disorderly hair gave him a warm feeling nonetheless—because that boy was him, that boy was his early years.

The past had gone out the door and faded into the far distance, but future days had yet to make their move. Lying there, he felt rather at a loss. But he had already bid farewell to that winsome boy as he wandered away, and in due course he would himself head off in a different direction.

So, in honor of his birthday, he stayed longer in bed, paying his respects to this milestone event that had just arrived and soon would depart. He had entered the station marking eighteen years of age, a station redolent of harmonica tunes.

At the end of the afternoon he was offered neither beer nor cake. He ate dinner as usual, then went to the kitchen to wash the dishes while his parents stood chatting on the balcony.

After he'd finished, he went into their bedroom and helped himself to one of his father's cigarettes. Right now the butt was lying by his pillow and he didn't feel like throwing it away just yet. And on the floor by his bed was a pile of cigarette ash. It was when he was smoking that he had seen the boy drifting away.

Today was his birthday, but nobody knew that. His parents had completely forgotten. He didn't blame them—it was his birthday, after all, not theirs.

Now, as that boy was gradually receding into the distance, he seemed to hear his own unfamiliar footsteps approaching. It was just that he hadn't yet knocked on the door.

He imagined how things would be when he woke up the following morning: when he opened his eyes he would see sunlight through the curtains, or if there was no sunlight he would see a band of gray. Maybe he would also hear the sound of water dripping from the eaves. But hopefully not, hopefully there would be bright sunshine and he would hear all kinds of sounds outside, sounds just as bright as the sunshine. The neighbors' four doves would be circling the roof delightfully, and he would get out of bed and stand by the window. But all of a sudden he sensed that tomorrow he would feel uneasy when he stood by the window, uneasy because of a new conviction that he was alone in the world.

Alone. That was the theme for the evening of his eighteenth birthday.

Now he had a distinct sense that something was happening to his eyes. They were rapidly becoming cold and sparkling. So he began to think about what he might see tomorrow. Even if what he saw tomorrow might well be just the same as what he'd seen before, he had a hunch things would be different.

3

Now he was on his way to Zhang Liang's house.

Bai Xue's signal and the middle-aged man's manner had left him baffled, but they also seemed a little droll. Later he thought perhaps he had misinterpreted. Before long, however, he felt he was absolutely right. There was no point in brooding about it, but he couldn't stop himself. It was all because of Bai Xue. A yellow blouse seemed to be stirring constantly in the dark shadows of thought.

He had entered a narrow alleyway whose high walls were decorated with moss, clumps of moss that seemed to have been pasted on like slogans. Underfoot, the alley had been laid with stone pavers that with the passage of time had grown unstable: when you stepped on them they would move up and down, and so it was as though he were walking down an alley that rocked back and forth. Above his head was a sky just as narrow as the alley, but cut into even finer lengths by electric cables.

He must now be outside Zhang Liang's house, he thought. There were two shiny copper rings on the pitch-black door. He felt himself grip the rings and push, and he listened as the aging door gave a creak of protest. A dank courtyard appeared before him. Zhang Liang's home was on the right.

Maybe it was at this moment that the yellow blouse finally departed from his mind, like a cloud that is dyed yellow by sunlight and then drifts away. Zhang Liang's image became clearer in his mind now that his home was so close.

"So it's you, dammit!" Zhang Liang said as he opened the door.

He stepped inside with a smile on his face, as though entering his own home.

They were classmates no longer, but friends. At the moment when they left school for good, he felt he had gained a friend, when before they were just classmates.

The door and window were closed, and the white curtain was drawn. On the curtain were painted an air gun and a catapult; a gun pellet and a catapult bolt were about to collide with each other. Zhang Liang himself had painted them.

At first he thought Zhang Liang wasn't home, but when he went up to the door he could hear whispering inside. He put his ear against the door, but he could not hear clearly what was being said. When he knocked, the sounds within came to an abrupt stop.

It was a good while before the door opened. Zhang Liang gave a start on seeing him, then muttered something or other and turned away. He could not help but hesitate before entering. Then he saw Zhu Qiao and Hansheng. They too gave a start on seeing him.

He found their manner off-putting. It was as though they did not recognize him, as though he should not have come at this particular time. His appearance, at any rate, had come as a surprise to them.

By the time he had taken a seat by the window, Zhang Liang was already lying on the bed. Zhang Liang seemed keen to say something, but all he did was smile. The smile was so unreadable, it left him spooked.

Zhu Qiao opened his mouth. "How did you know we were here?" he asked.

Zhu Qiao's question was even more unnerving than Zhang Liang's smile. He did not know how to answer. He had come to see Zhang Liang, but now it was Zhu Qiao asking the questions.

Hansheng was lying on the sofa with his eyes closed. It looked as though he had been sleeping for at least a couple of hours.

When he shot another glance at Zhu Qiao, he had his head buried in a magazine.

Only Zhang Liang was looking at him as before, but with a glint in his eye that made him uneasy. He felt that to Zhang Liang he was as boring as the ceiling.

"Yesterday was my birthday," he told them.

Hearing this, they jumped to their feet and cursed him angrily. Why had he not let them know? They all stuck their hands in their pockets, but the money they came up with was only enough to buy a single bottle of beer.

"I'll go get it." So saying, Zhang Liang went out the door.

Zhang Liang was still looking at him, and he didn't know what to do. His sudden appearance had put them out of sorts, and it seemed as though they had been discussing something they didn't want to tell him. This was a sad discovery to make on such a lovely, sunny morning.

Suddenly he thought of Bai Xue. *She actually had not gone far, she had simply hidden behind a utility pole. She could appear at any moment and block his escape route. That look of hers was so hard to figure out.*

"What's the matter?"

It seemed that Zhang Liang had asked this question, but maybe it was Zhu Qiao or Hansheng. He wished he were somewhere else.

4

He stood in front of a dusty building and looked up at one particular window that lorded it over the others, gaping like the mouth of a corpse. A coal-briquette stove stood on the windowsill, issuing a plume of dense smoke: the window served as a chimney.

Entering the building was like inching one's way into a dark cave. With his feet he felt for the staircase; then he carefully began to climb. It puzzled him that his footsteps could be so hollow. Then he heard another set of footsteps, equally hollow, and at first he thought it was simply an echo. But the noise was slowly descending, and it faded away just as it reached him. Only then did he become aware that somebody was standing in front of him and blocking his way. He could hear the man breathing heavily—and the man must have heard the noise too. Then the man reached into a pocket and groped about. The rustling noise unsettled him, and he felt a sudden impulse to knock the man off balance and shove him down the stairs. But the man's hand was already out, and then he heard a click and saw a flame burning. It lit up half the man's face, leaving the other half in a sinister darkness. That single, half-closed eye made him shiver. Then the man passed him on his left and trotted down the stairs with a tip-tap rhythm, as if playing the organ. He seemed to recall at this moment who the man was, reminded of the middle-aged smoker underneath the plane tree.

Soon after, he stood in front of a door on the fifth floor and gave it a little kick. There was no reaction inside. So he put his ear to the door, only to find to his amazement that an iron nail was poking into his ear. The nail had been driven into the door, he realized, and, groping with his fingers, he found that four other nails were embedded in the door at precisely the same height where his ear had been pressing.

The door now suddenly swung open and a beam of light surged out like a wave, dazzling him. This was followed by a cry of delight. "Hey, it's you!"

Once his eyes had adjusted to the glare, he saw that Zhang Liang was standing before him. When he thought of how he had left his home shortly before, only to run into him again here, he was stunned. What's more, Zhang Liang's cheerful expression was in stark contrast to his manner earlier.

"Why don't you come in?"

He went in, and found that Zhu Qiao and Hansheng were there. One was sitting in a chair and the other was sitting on the table; both looked at him merrily.

A nameless anxiety surged up in his heart. He smiled awkwardly. "Where is he?" he asked.

"Who?" the three of them asked, almost in unison.

"Yazhou," he replied. After saying this, he was puzzled: Why did they need to ask? It was Yazhou's apartment, after all.

"Didn't you see him?" Zhang Liang seemed surprised. "Didn't you meet on the stairs?"

How would Zhang Liang know that he would meet someone on the stairs? Could that person have been Yazhou? He saw how the three of them looked at one another and chuckled. So he concluded that the man had just left and was not Yazhou.

He sat down on a chair by the window, the window where

a briquette stove had been burning, but now was no longer there. There was sunlight, though, and it shone on his hair. So then he imagined the color of his hair at this moment, and he thought it would surely look weird.

Zhang Liang and the others were still smiling, and it seemed they had been doing so for a long time—they had been smiling even before he entered. So now the amused expressions on their faces were fading away.

Suddenly he was racked with worry. As he came in, to mask his surprise he had forced himself to smile, and now the smile was glued onto his face. It peeved him that he couldn't get rid of it.

"What's the matter?"

He heard Zhu Qiao or Hansheng ask this question, and then saw Zhang Liang looking at him quizzically.

"He's changed a bit." Again it was Zhu Qiao or Hansheng. But the voice seemed unfamiliar.

"Is it me you're talking about?" He looked at Zhang Liang. His own voice also sounded strange.

Zhang Liang seemed to nod.

Now they appeared to be rubbing their faces with their hands, until their frozen smiles were rubbed away. They began to look at him soberly, the same way that the math teacher with the glasses looked at him. But he felt there was something unreal about it.

He was rather upset, because he didn't know what they had been saying before he came in and he wanted very much to know.

"When did you get here?"

What sounded like Yazhou's voice drifted toward him, as though from outside the window. But then he saw Yazhou for real standing right in front of him, and he couldn't help but give a start. He had not registered at all the fact that Yazhou had come in, and it was as though he had never left. Yazhou was now looking at him with a grin, the very same grin he had seen on Zhang Liang and the others' faces.

"What's up with you?" It was Yazhou who asked. They were all asking this. Then Yazhou turned around, and he saw that perplexing smile reappear on the faces of Zhang Liang and the others. Yazhou, he thought, must be smiling in just the same way.

He didn't want to look at them anymore, and so he looked out the window. He saw a briquette stove on the windowsill opposite, but no smoke was issuing from it. Then the stove suddenly disappeared and he saw a girl with her back to him, and then she too vanished. So then he felt there was nothing more to see, but he didn't feel like turning around right away.

He heard one of them stand up and move about, and soon a burst of whispers and stifled laughter issued from the balcony. Only then did he turn his head, to find Zhang Liang and Co. gone. Yazhou, still seated as before, was idly toying with a cigarette lighter.

5

When he came out of Zhang Liang's house, a white-haired old lady was standing in the gloomy alleyway shouting someone's name. He didn't know whether or not that person was her grandson, but it seemed she was calling, "Yazhou."

So he decided to go to Yazhou's place. Although Yazhou

was his friend, he seldom got together with Zhang Liang and the others. The antagonism between Yazhou and Zhang Liang and Co. often put him in an awkward position and made things difficult on both sides.

He didn't head directly for Yazhou's apartment, but ambled slowly down some street or other. Piles of bricks and heaps of sand lined the street at regular intervals, and a steamroller drove back and forth in a seemingly offhand manner. Walking down the street felt like threading one's way through a construction site.

For a while he leaned against a pile of bricks and watched the steamroller, which was just as bored as he was. Its huge wheels thumped dully as they leveled the surface.

But this just irritated him: he found the noise unbearable. So he let his legs start moving. The movement felt comical, all the more so when his arms started moving back and forth as though they were walking too.

Later—he didn't know exactly what time, but he knew it was later—he seemed to be standing in the doorway of a shop that sold tobacco and candy, or possibly it sold silk. Precisely what kind of place it was did not matter; the main thing was that he saw a lot of different colors. Most likely he was standing in between two shops, but in fact the two shops were not adjacent to each other, so maybe it was that he had stood outside first one shop and then the other. In any case he saw a lot of colors, a riot of different hues.

At this moment a comfortable feeling surged up in his heart, so suddenly as to take him by surprise. Then he caught sight of Bai Xue.

He saw her walk along the street, trailing a black shadow. He thought that when she got next to the plane tree she might come to a stop and maybe throw him a glance, a meaningful look that he would find perplexing. That was what happened when he saw her the last time, and he didn't know why he was repeating it all.

But she really did go over to the plane tree and come to a stop, and she did throw him a glance, and her glance did hint at the same thing it had earlier. And then she hurried away, just as before.

He was staggered to find that his supposition would prove so true. And then he tensed up, for he felt as though a middle-aged man was leaning against the plane tree. He quickly looked all around, but did not see him. But he did spot a suspicious silhouette disappearing into an alleyway. The entry to the alleyway looked as dark as the mouth of a well, and it filled him with dread. But he took off in pursuit nonetheless. He seemed to hope—and at the same time fear—that the silhouette belonged to the middle-aged man.

At the entry to the alley he almost ran into someone, a middle-aged man who muttered something and then walked away. He was heading in exactly the same direction that he had been taking to go to Yazhou's house. Why wasn't the man going somewhere else? He suspected that this man was the one whose silhouette he had just seen: after dodging into the alley he had come out again, pretending to be completely uninvolved. It seemed the man knew that he was planning to visit Yazhou, and so he was heading that way too.

After proceeding some twenty meters, he noticed, the man came to a stop and glanced around in all directions, resting his eyes on him briefly, only to look away at once. The man was monitoring his movements, he sensed, and was simply pretending to look around in order to disarm suspicion.

The man remained standing there, but no longer looked his way. The man's head was slightly tilted in his direction, however, so he felt that he was still in the man's line of vision. He stood where he was and just stared at him.

Another middle-aged man came over and said a few words to the first one, and the two men walked off together. After going a little way, the second man turned his head and threw him a glance. His companion patted him on the shoulder, and he did not look back again.

6

Now it was dusk. He stood on the balcony and gazed at the building opposite. Some of its windows were bright, and some were dark. The bright windows seemed to him like a series of rectangular lights, and together they formed an intriguing picture: not symmetrical, perhaps, but perfectly proportioned. He tried to think of what the picture looked like, but couldn't come up with an answer. This was because whenever he thought of something, two windows would suddenly brighten and the composition would be critically altered. So he had to start from the beginning again.

Just now, when he was in the kitchen washing the dishes, all of a sudden he had become aware of a distinct possibility that his parents were discussing him. He had pricked up his ears to listen. Faint though the voices were, there was no doubt that he was being talked about. After a little hesitation he had edged closer, but by then they were on another subject and he couldn't make much sense of what they were saying. It had seemed to him that their conversation was strained: evidently they were having to rack their brains to find words that they would understand intuitively but that would leave him none the wiser.

He had suddenly felt as though he was a barrier that inhibited communication between them.

"Have you finished the washing up?" his father had asked.

"No." He shook his head.

His father looked at him with disapproval. His mother had then struck up a conversation with someone on the adjacent balcony. "Are you pretty much all ready now?" she asked.

"How about you?" the neighbor responded.

His mother did not reply, but switched to another topic.

Then he had gone back to the kitchen, and this time tried to make as little noise as possible when washing the dishes. Soon he again seemed to hear them talking about him. Their voices began to get louder, and several times he heard his name mentioned, but then they appeared to realize their mistake and promptly lowered their voices.

He put the dishes back in the cabinet, then went out onto the balcony and leaned against the railing in the corner opposite them. Despite that, he still sensed that he was getting in their way.

They clearly found his reappearance displeasing, because again his father had a bone to pick with him. "You've got to stop being so aimless," he said. "You ought to study."

So he had no choice but to leave. Once back in his room, he picked up a book. He didn't know the title—all he knew was that it had words printed on its pages.

On the balcony, his parents continued their discussion, punctuating it with chuckles. They chuckled without restraint.

He felt uneasy, and after a moment of hesitation he took his book and went out onto the balcony.

This time his father had said nothing, but had eyed him silently, just like his mother. Even without looking at them he could tell what kind of expression was in their eyes.

It was then that dusk had arrived, then that he gazed listlessly at the building opposite. He had been eager to hear just what they were saying. But all he could see was a mysterious picture.

Later he gave a start, because he discovered that he was standing by the door to their bedroom. The door was tightly shut. They were no longer talking without a pause as they had been earlier—they now spoke at intervals and their words were difficult to make out. The only two that came across plainly were "April Third." But he was hard put to discern their import.

Suddenly the door opened and his father emerged. "What are you doing here?" he asked testily. He saw that his mother was looking at him with feigned astonishment. There was no mistaking it—her surprise was just a performance.

He didn't know how to answer his father's question. He just looked at him dumbly, then walked off. He heard his father grumbling as the bedroom door closed behind him.

He went back to his own room and lay down in bed. Now everything around was in darkness, but he felt his eyes were glowing bright. There was noise outside, some of it close by and some of it far away, but by the time it reached his room it had all become a monotonous hum.

7

According to the arrangement he had imagined the night before, today he ought to wake up at 8:30. Then, after seeing the sun filter through the curtains and linger on the socks that were hanging on the footboard, he would get out of bed and hear a knock on the door.

Before the old wall clock emitted its lonely chime, he had been sunk in a deep whirlpool of confused slumber. Even in his sleep, however, he had heard various noises outside his room, and the noises had simply added to his lassitude. When the old clock chimed, it changed everything, like a light that comes on suddenly in a darkened room. So then he woke, to find himself covered in sweat.

Wearily, he propped himself up. Sitting there in bed, he felt a lot more relaxed. At the same time he glanced at the clock: 8:30. He leaned back against the headboard and began to think about something or other. Suddenly he gave a start and threw another glance at the clock: he was now convinced that 8:30 had indeed been his wake-up time. He looked at the sunlight, which was lingering on his smelly socks just as expected. All this was in keeping with the arrangement he had made in his imagination the night before.

What should follow was a knock on the door. But that should happen after he got out of bed. Even though the first two points had been verified, he was somewhat doubtful whether the knock on the door would materialize. He lounged on the bed, unwilling to get up, for in fact he wanted to limit the pos-

sibility of hearing the knock after he got out of bed. If someone was really going to knock on the door, he would prefer to
hear the knock when lying in bed.

So he stayed in bed until 9:30. His parents left for work
at 7:30, so he could listen very single-mindedly to the clock
without any danger that he would be distracted by other
noises in the house.

By 9:30 he felt he was not going to hear a knock—that was
last night's imagination, after all. He decided to get up.

After getting out of bed he first opened the window, and
the sunshine burst in boldly, accompanied by a breeze and
some noise. The noise annoyed him, because to his ears it
seemed remote and unreal.

On his way to the kitchen he heard a knock. It was after
he had gotten up, and he turned pale with astonishment that
things had turned out just as he had envisioned.

When last night he imagined hearing a knock on the door,
he did not turn pale but simply felt a little bemused; he'd then
gone over and opened the door. The time for surprise would
have been after he opened the door, because that was when
a middle-aged man (the smoker who had leaned against the
plane tree) entered the room without saying a word.

He would have challenged the visitor, obviously. "Can I
help you?"

But the man ignored his question. Instead the man came
closer and closer, forcing him to take several steps backward,
until he was up against the wall and could not retreat any farther, at which point the man stood still. He had sensed that
something would surely happen next. But what precisely was
going to happen, he had not been able to imagine the night
before.

Now, when he heard the noise, he couldn't help but tense up. He stood still, as if unwilling to open the door. The knocks became louder and louder, making him feel the visitor was sure he was inside, and given the visitor's confidence on this score, he felt there was no way to avoid all that was about to happen. At the same time, from another angle, he was keen to find out just what would transpire.

He opened the door and was startled (just as projected in last night's imaginings), because the man was knocking on the door on the opposite side of the landing (an act different from what he had imagined). He saw a sturdy figure, and, judging from that, he thought the person had to be a middle-aged man (the man's age, then, was consistent with what he had imagined). But was it the man so closely associated with the plane tree? He found it hard to make a determination. It seemed that he was the man, and also that he wasn't.

8

The shop's display window functioned somewhat like a mirror. He walked back and forth in front of it, turning his head sideways and looking at his reflection. But the moving image was blurry, and impaired by the items on display.

As he stood in front of the pharmacy window, he noticed that three boxes of herbal extract ingeniously formed his abdomen, while his shoulders were replaced by a triangle of bottled calcium tablets. The apex of the triangle ended precisely underneath his nose, so his eyes were not compromised. He looked at the reflection of his eyes, and it was very much as though another pair of eyes was watching him.

Then he walked over to the window of the department store. There his abdomen was restored to him, but his chest was obstructed by a child's shirt. And his head disappeared, its place occupied instead by a pair of swimming trunks. But his hands were free: when he stretched out his right hand it could touch the bell of a bicycle, and when he stretched out his left it almost made contact with a badminton racket, but not quite.

Just at this moment the window reflected several hazy human shapes, also interrupted by items on display. He saw half a head saying something to most of a face, as several legs shifted about, and a few shoulders as well. Then he saw a complete face appear, but without a neck—there was a red bra where the neck should have been. Detecting a furtiveness in several of the fragmented reflections, he spun around, only to see a number of people standing on the opposite sidewalk pointing at him and making remarks.

Because he had turned so suddenly, they all appeared a bit flustered. "What are you doing?" one of them asked.

He gave a start, for he could see they were all looking at him in amusement and he couldn't tell which one of them had asked the question. He felt he didn't know who they were, although they looked familiar.

"Are you waiting for someone?"

Again he could not discern which of them had spoken. But it was true he was waiting for someone. How would they know that, though? He was taken aback.

Seeing that he didn't react, they seemed a bit embarrassed.

They talked in low voices and then left together. Strangely, they did not look back.

He began to walk. What had just happened was puzzling, and now the stuff in the window seemed as dull as dishwater. So he switched his attention to the street. There were not many pedestrians about; those that he did see were half in light and half in darkness.

"Why didn't you answer?"

Zhu Qiao's voice sounded in his ears and gave him a start. Now Zhu Qiao was standing in front of him. Zhu Qiao seemed to have suddenly emerged from hiding, and he was rendered speechless.

"Why didn't you answer them?" Zhu Qiao asked once more.

He looked at him in confusion. "Who are they?" he asked.

Zhu Qiao gave an exaggerated expression of surprise. "They're your classmates."

He seemed to remember now: they were indeed his former classmates. But when he saw Zhu Qiao smiling so comically, he couldn't help but doubt that this was so.

Zhu Qiao patted his shoulder warmly. "What are you doing here?"

He found this familiarity rather excessive. But that was a minor issue—the big question was why he was asking this.

"Are you waiting for someone?"

It was obvious: Zhu Qiao had some obscure connection with those other people just now, and it seemed they were all concerned about who he was waiting for.

"No, I'm not."

"Well, why have you been standing here all this time?"

This was a shock. Clearly Zhu Qiao had been watching him

from some hidden vantage point. So it was pointless to argue that he wasn't waiting for anyone.

"What's the matter?" Zhu Qiao asked.

He could see that Zhu Qiao was on edge—having noticed his wary manner, no doubt. Uneasily he turned his head away, and he contrived to take a casual look around.

It was then he realized with surprise just how many people were paying attention to them. Practically everyone in the street was acting strangely, he felt. Even though their surveillance of him might take different forms, just a single glance revealed their inner secret.

Opposite him were three people standing in a cluster and chatting as they kept him under observation, and similar situations unfolded to his right and left. People walking along the street would cast a glance in his direction, then quickly avert their gaze as though fearful he would notice. He suspected that Zhu Qiao was talking to him now as a way of diverting his attention. He discovered that those people who seemed to be strangers to one another turned out to be slowly coalescing into a group as they walked. Although they soon separated again, he knew that they had had time to exchange remarks— brief remarks, perhaps, but concerning him.

Later, when he looked back, Zhu Qiao was nowhere to be seen. He had no recollection of when he had left.

9

The brawny figure in front of him reminded him of a stone monument. When he had seen such a monument and what exactly it was like were not questions he was inclined to consider in more detail. What was more to the point was that this figure was knocking on the door. And he knocked with care, using two knuckles, but the noise was very loud, as though he were pounding on it with both fists. The man's feet were not being employed, but if they were—he supposed—the outcome would surely be ugly.

He stood by the door, waiting, it seemed, for this man to turn around. He tried to guess what a frontal view of him would be like. All he could be sure of was that he would look more complicated from the front than from the back. Would he turn out to be the middle-aged man who had leaned against the plane tree?

But the man continued to knock on the door, with a beat so steady and mechanical it sounded like the rhythm of a lathe.

Given his interest in seeing the man's face—an interest he could not contain—he decided to say something to him. There was no other way.

"There's nobody home," he said.

The man turned around, finally exposing his face. His front was not as solidly built as his back, but his eyebrows were short and unnervingly bushy, so it looked almost as though he had four eyes. He could not readily establish whether this was the man who had leaned against the plane tree, but he was disinclined to rule out the possibility.

"There's nobody home," he repeated.

The man looked at him as though looking at a door. "How do you know there's nobody home?"

"If there were, they would have opened up by now."

"Would they open up if I didn't knock?" the man asked mockingly.

"But if there's nobody home, they won't open up no matter how much you knock."

"But if there *is* somebody there, they *will* open up if I keep knocking."

He took a couple of steps back and shut the door. He found the exchange perplexing. The knocking on the door resumed. But he didn't want to pay it any attention, so he went into the kitchen, where a couple of fried dough-sticks awaited him. His mother had bought them that morning, in keeping with her usual practice. Left on top of a bowl, they were now drooping at both ends. He picked them up and ate them, at the same time picturing how straight they would have been when just purchased.

After he had finished, a strange thought struck him: the dough-sticks might have been poisoned. And soon he realized he was quite convinced that this was the case, because he could feel a discomfort in his stomach, though it stopped well short of acute pain. He stood still, waiting for the disturbance to develop further. But after a little while it subsided and his stomach reverted to calm. He stood a bit longer, and finally heaved a sigh of relief, as though unburdened of a heavy weight.

The man was still pounding on the door. And the more he

pounded, the more it sounded like the man was knocking on *his* door. He began to suspect that that was really what was happening. So he stood by the door and listened intently. Yes, the door was being knocked on—he seemed to feel the door trembling. He took a deep breath and threw the door open.

What he saw was the neighbors' door slamming shut. It must have just been opened, because the burly figure was no longer there.

10

If last night's imaginings were to be fulfilled, he would see Bai Xue here again today. This time she would give no clear signal. She would walk past him as though he weren't there and not even look at him. But that too would be a signal. So, pretending to be out for a stroll, he would follow close on her heels. What would happen next he had not been able to imagine.

The girl standing behind the writing supplies counter had long hair that fell to her shoulders. She was looking at him as if spellbound.

Zhu Qiao had disappeared all of a sudden, as though in a jump cut in a movie, and now he found himself in a very suspect environment. He noticed the girl's look only after he had turned in her direction.

Because he had turned around so quickly, the girl appeared to have been taken by surprise. First she tensely shifted her gaze, then turned her back to him and began to count ink bottles and coloring boxes as though checking the inventory.

He hadn't expected that people would monitor him also

from behind his back, and he felt a tremor of alarm. But she was different from the others, after all, for she seemed panic-stricken when discovered, whereas they were able to feign complete innocence.

He moved slowly toward her. She kept on checking her inventory, but she could sense that he was standing next to her—she could hear him breathing. So she seemed all the more nervous and her shoulders began to quiver. She tried to avoid him, moving off to one side, her back to him.

Now he spoke up, in a voice both firm and calm. "Why are you watching me?" he asked.

She froze, and her shoulders trembled acutely.

"Answer me," he said. But his tone was cordial.

She hesitated a moment, then turned around and said bleakly, "They made me do it."

"I know." He nodded. "But why do they want to monitor me?"

She opened her mouth, but no sound came out. She looked around fearfully.

Without even checking, he knew that everyone in the shop was now looking at her threateningly.

"Don't be afraid," he murmured.

She hesitated a moment, then summoned her courage to say, "I'll tell you."

He stood at the entrance to the shop and watched her intently. She kept on doing the inventory for quite some time before turning around, but when she realized he was still looking at her, she at once became flustered. This time she did not turn her back to him, but moved to the other end of the counter. She was no longer in his line of vision and all he saw were neat rows of ink bottles and coloring boxes.

He thought about whether or not to go back in, march up
to her, and conduct the kind of conversation he had just imagined. But he lacked the sangfroid that he had possessed in his
mock situation, and she clearly was not as gentle and kind-
hearted as the girl in his hypothesis. For this reason he lacked
confidence in the outcome of a conversation that would be
absolutely real and would lack even the slightest imaginative
coloring.

He stood indecisively at the entrance, as chaotic footsteps
sounded behind him. He could vividly imagine the look in the
eyes of those people tailing him. At this moment he had his
back to them, and they would be free to watch him without
the least scruple and even gesture to one another. But, he
thought, if he suddenly turned around, they would be taken
completely by surprise. He was pleased with himself for hitting on this plan, and immediately put it into action.

But when he turned around, he did not achieve the antici-
pated effect. A quick survey of the surrounding scene failed
to uncover anyone watching him. They had read his mind,
and this he found infuriating. They're getting more cunning,
he thought.

But Bai Xue did appear.

According to his imagined scenario, Bai Xue would come
ambling along the street (from either direction). But now Bai
Xue was coming over the bridge. Although the particulars dif-
fered, his overall projection had again proved correct.

As Bai Xue came down the bridge, she did not look his way.
But he knew she had seen him, and he knew that she knew
he had seen her. When she did not look his way, it was so as to
avoid notice. She sauntered down the bridge very coolly and

then walked off in the opposite direction from him. Bai Xue's casualness impressed him deeply, and he began to follow her.

Bai Xue stood out conspicuously among the pedestrians because she was wearing a bright red corduroy jacket. He knew there was something significant about her choice of attire and he appreciated her attention to detail. But immediately he realized that it was silly of him to stare at her, because that could so easily give him away.

11

He had to think hard before he could recall the exchange between his mother and the neighbor on the balcony the previous afternoon.

"Are you pretty much all ready now?" she had asked.

"How about you?" was the rejoinder.

Just now, while still a little way from home, he could see a boy lying on the neighbors' balcony and gazing at the street below. At the same time he saw that the door to his own balcony was open, so he concluded that his parents were home. As soon as the boy saw him, he turned around and ran indoors. At first he did not give any thought to that, but when he got to the foot of the stairs and was about to go up, he saw the boy a second time, and this time he was pointing a toy pistol at him. Then, in a flash, the boy darted into his apartment and the door slammed with a bang.

It was only when he got home that he realized his parents were not there. He looked carefully in all the rooms, and on the easy chair in his parents' bedroom he saw a nylon shopping bag. Without question, his parents had come back, because at lunchtime he had seen his mother go out with that bag. He remembered that his father had asked, "What do you need that for?" He couldn't remember now how his mother answered. But that wasn't important—what mattered was that he had verified that his parents had returned before he did.

What required consideration now was where his parents had gone. He could not help thinking of that highly suspicious knocking on the door by the middle-aged man. For this reason the neighbors next door also seemed to him highly suspicious. And even their child gave him cause to be wary. Although the boy was only six years old, he was just as sneaky as a grown-up.

It was obvious that his parents were next door. Now, when he closed his eyes, he could picture them sitting with the neighbors and discussing things.

"Are you pretty much all ready now?"

"How about you?"

(What was worth noting was that they were preparing something. He could feel a twinge of foreboding, but could not imagine the particulars.)

The boy had been sent onto the balcony to observe whether or not he was on his way back. Later the boy had appeared at the doorway, and when he started going upstairs the boy had slammed the door. This noise had to be significant: it would tell them that he was on his way up.

He knew what he had to do now. He had to verify this hypothesis. And the means of verification were simple: he just needed to open the door, stand in the doorway, and keep his eyes fixed on the door opposite.

His glance would not be the timid glance of before—his glance would make it clear that he had seen through their scheme. And so, when his parents emerged, they would be totally taken aback.

They would expect the door to be closed and him to be inside. So they'd put on a show of being at ease, as if they had just come up the stairs, unaware he was standing in the doorway.

First they'd be astonished, and then embarrassed, because it was all so sudden and they hadn't sufficient time to prepare a cover-up. Sure, they'd be quick to assume a relaxed posture, but there was no way they could mask their discomfiture.

12

The red jacket maintained such a steady distance from him— always twenty meters ahead—it was as though it were not really moving. This was because Bai Xue walked with such even steps.

Bai Xue continued along the same street, and that was dangerous, because he was more and more conscious that the bystanders were paying attention to them. He had observed that several people passed right next to Bai Xue, only to turn back to look at her, and then, as though noticing something, they took a look at him too. After he brushed past them, he felt as though they took a few steps and then seemed to turn round and follow him. He did not turn his head—at this time he must absolutely avoid doing that. Just hearing footsteps close behind told him all he needed to know. There was no longer a clear pattern to the footsteps, which showed there were all the more people shadowing him.

But Bai Xue kept on walking along the street. He knew exactly how far this street extended, and was aware that before long it would peter out into a dirt road. The dirt road, which skirted a river on one side and open land on the other, led eventually to the crematorium, whose tall chimney gave one the feeling that the long, spindly dirt road was now suddenly standing erect.

Bai Xue had not yet gotten to the start of the dirt road, but she wasn't that far away. She hesitated at the entry to several alleys, but carried on straight ahead. Only he could sense that hesitation of hers. Clearly she had noticed she was being watched.

Just at this moment Bai Xue came to a stop. If she didn't stop now, she would miss the chance altogether, because she was nearing the end of the street. Bai Xue entered a shop, a little convenience store that stocked the same items as all the shops she had already passed. It was obvious that making a purchase was not her aim.

He slowed his pace, knowing there was an alley about ten meters on this side of the shop, a very narrow alley. He moved forward cautiously. There seemed to be fewer people in the street now. He observed that up ahead only two people were watching him: one walking toward him, the other standing by the door of a waste recycling depot.

As he passed the shop, he did not look inside, but he began to feel that the footsteps following him had dwindled in number, and when he reached the alley he heard no footsteps at all. Bai Xue's ruse had worked perfectly, he thought. But the man outside the recycling depot was still looking at him.

He slipped into the alley.

Here the sunlight was blocked by the high walls on both sides, and no sooner had he stepped inside than he was hit by a wave of clammy air. The passageway ran straight and long, like a path through a dense forest. He walked on quietly, into the depths of the alley. At intervals on both sides there appeared still smaller alleys, so narrow they could accommodate only a single person, and they were quiet and empty. The alley was a full hundred meters in length. He walked all the way to the end before turning around, and from that distance the alley entrance looked like a narrow slit. Seeing no one, he couldn't help but breathe a sigh of relief, because that meant that for the time being nobody was watching him. He stood waiting for Bai Xue to appear.

Before long Bai Xue completed a graceful turn and entered through the slit. As he watched, the bright red jacket turned a darker red. Bai Xue strolled casually, with footsteps as enchanting as the sound of water drops hitting the ground. There was brightness behind her, and so as she walked toward him her body was bathed in light.

All of this was consistent with his projection, and now he knew everything that would happen next.

But at that moment two people suddenly entered from a side alley and walked shoulder to shoulder toward the street. Their bodies blocked his view of Bai Xue.

What shocked him was that one of them was his father, and the other seemed to be the man who had leaned against the plane tree, smoking. Walking with their backs to him, they did not notice him. They were discussing something, and though they kept their voices low he could hear a snatch of their conversation.

"What day?" It had to be the middle-aged man who asked this.

"April Third," his father replied.

He could not catch anything else they said. As they proceeded forward, the two silhouettes slowly contracted and the slit slowly expanded, but still they blocked his view of Bai Xue. Their footsteps were very loud, as though they were banging on a table with their hands. Then they reached the slit and went separate ways, his father to the right, the other man to the left.

But he did not see Bai Xue.

13

His parents, it turned out, came up the stairs. He knew it was them as soon as he heard their footsteps.

Without a doubt, when he went into the apartment, they had come out of the door opposite and quietly gone downstairs. Otherwise the boy's slamming of the door would have lost its significance. And so, when he was standing in the doorway, his parents were already downstairs.

Now they were coming upstairs (they had much more experience than he did, after all). He saw how they looked at him in surprise, but it wasn't the kind of surprise he had been expecting.

"What are you doing standing in the doorway?"

His father's mouth had moved, and this sound emerged from inside. Then two human figures came to a halt in front of him. He noticed that the buttons on his father's jacket were different from those on his mother's.

"What's the matter?"

It was his mother's voice, different from the first one. It was like cotton.

Suddenly he felt he was blocking his parents' path, and so he hurriedly moved to one side. Now he noticed that his parents exchanged a look, a look that was rich with meaning. They said nothing more, and after entering the apartment they each went their own way, his mother to the kitchen, his father to the bedroom.

But he didn't know what to do: he would seem so clueless just standing there. It dawned on him that there was something foolish about his stance just now, because his parents must have known what was on his mind.

His father emerged from the bedroom and walked toward the kitchen. Halfway there he stopped and said, "Close the door."

He put out his hand and closed the door, listening as that simple sound rapidly disappeared.

A moment or two after his father entered the kitchen he said something else: "Take out the trash."

As he picked up the dustpan he gave a sigh of relief: he no longer felt quite so helpless. He opened the door to find the neighbors' son standing on the landing, toy pistol in hand. Cockily, the boy aimed the gun at him. He knew why the boy was so pleased with himself, even at such a tender age.

He stepped forward and grabbed the boy's weapon. "My parents were over at your place just now, weren't they?" he asked.

The boy wasn't the least bit afraid. With a quick tug he grabbed the gun back, at the same time shouting, "No, they weren't."

So, even the kid's well trained, he thought.

14

He stood there for a long time, his eyes on the slit, as though he were at the bottom of a deep well and watching its mouth. Occasionally someone slipped past the entry to the alley, like a large bird sailing over the well with a flap of its wings.

He proceeded forward with caution, and the sound of his footsteps bounced off the walls and tapped against his toes. Peering down the side alleys, he found they were all equally empty of people. As he reached the fourth side alley he saw a utility pole in front of him and realized he was now very close to where Hansheng lived.

Entering the side alley, one found oneself on an untidy, ramshackle path that sloped slightly upward. At the fourth door there was no need to knock—one could simply push the door open, revealing a small courtyard, its four corners swathed in moss. Then one followed a dark, unpaved passageway, skirting a small water-filled pit, to reach Hansheng's door.

Hansheng's house was much like Zhang Liang's, and so the scene in which they were hiding in the room and whispering to one another vividly came to mind.

What now needed serious consideration was this: At what point could Bai Xue have disappeared? But to follow this thought to its logical conclusion would only heighten his unease. Because he felt she had disappeared right here. Moreover—if he continued to pursue this line of thought— she would have come to a stop outside the fourth door, would have pushed the door open and walked along the dark passageway. So Bai Xue should be sitting in Hansheng's house right now.

He felt that this premise must be very close to reality, and so his disquiet grew all the more real. At the same time it made him take a first step toward Hansheng's home. What he needed now was not imagination, but verification. He came to a stop outside the fourth door.

Soon he had skirted that sinister pit and was knocking on the crude door. Before he did that, he conducted a manual inspection. There were no nails on Hansheng's door. So he could knock on it without any qualms.

The door opened quickly, but just a crack. Then Hansheng's head appeared in the opening. It was motionless, as though suspended in the air.

Light from the room spilled out and there was a strange look in Hansheng's eyes. He heard Hansheng ask tensely, "Who is it?"

He hesitated. "It's me," he answered.

"Oh, it's you." Only now did the door open fully.

Hansheng's voice took him off guard, because he had not planned on hearing such a loud voice.

He did not find Bai Xue in the room. But as he entered, he seemed to catch a whiff of scent. He couldn't tell if it came from a girl's hair or from a girl's face, but he was certain it came from a girl. He thought Bai Xue had maybe already left, but immediately he ruled this out. If she had left, she would have had to go back the way she'd come, but he had not seen her.

Hansheng led him to his room, which was spotlessly clean. He didn't let him see the other two rooms. The door to one of the rooms was open, and the door to the other was tightly closed.

"What brings you here?" Hansheng put on a show of being casual.

He felt this question inappropriate, for in the past he had been a frequent visitor. But now, he thought, the question perhaps made sense.

"I'm reading something interesting," Hansheng said.

He ignored this remark. He hadn't come here to engage in desultory chitchat with Hansheng; he had another purpose in mind. So he listened with great concentration.

"It's really well written."

He heard a slight noise, like that of something falling on the floor. He tried to determine its source, and decided that it came from the room whose door was closed.

Hansheng said nothing more. He picked up a magazine and started flipping through it.

He was glad of that, for this way he could concentrate on listening. But Hansheng made a lot of noise as he flipped through the magazine, and this was annoying. No doubt he was doing it deliberately.

Even so, at intervals he could still hear some slight movements. Now he was certain that Bai Xue was inside. She had concealed herself when Hansheng called out, and his shout had drowned out the sound of her closing the door.

Evidently, when Bai Xue ducked into the shop earlier, that was to give him the slip. It would drive him to despair if he discovered that she was in league with them, but he could not be absolutely sure this was the case.

He saw Hansheng close the door that was still open, as though he had remembered something. Too late, he thought.

15

Never before had he observed so intently the sky turning dark as he did this evening.

After dinner he didn't wash the dishes but went out onto the balcony instead. What was odd was that his father did not reprimand him. He heard his mother go into the kitchen, and soon there was a clatter of bowls and plates.

Rosy light sprinkled itself everywhere, like fresh blood, and the sun fell slowly like a punctured balloon, disappearing behind the building opposite. Then he heard his father come over, and soon he felt a hand pat his hair.

"Why not go out for a walk?" his father said pleasantly.

Inwardly he gave a cold smile. His father's affability was a sham. He shook his head. Now he felt his mother join them.

The three of them stood in silence for a moment, and then his father asked once more, "How about a walk?" Again he shook his head.

His parents exchanged a glance and then left the balcony. Soon he heard a door shut and knew that they had gone out.

He lowered his gaze, and soon he saw their silhouettes slowly moving away.

Then the family of three who lived next door appeared—also walking down the street at a leisurely pace. At almost the same time he saw other neighbors come out onto the sidewalk, all heading in the same direction, pretending to go for a stroll.

"Spring is here—let's go for a walk," he heard someone say. This comment was intended for his ears, he thought. It was just as fake as his father's invitation just now.

It was patently obvious: while pretending to be out for a stroll, they had set off on their mission, and they would all gather somewhere to confer, and no doubt their discussion would focus on him.

Some residents had not left, but were still standing on their balconies. That was part of the plan, he thought—to leave a few people to watch him.

He raised his head and scanned the sky. It seemed to be turning pale. The ruddy clouds had dispersed and the deep blue had receded into the far distance. It was the first time he had noticed that the sky turns pale after sunset. But the paleness was temporary, and behind it the blue could still dimly be seen. Then the blue gradually deepened, at the same time slowly spreading out of the paleness. That was how the sky got dark.

He remained on the balcony even after the sky turned black. He saw that in the building opposite only four windows were lit up. Then he looked down at his own block, which had five windows that were illuminated. Only then did he go in and turn on the light.

As he slowly descended the staircase, the thought occurred to him that perhaps those dark windows were watching him too. So when he reached the ground floor he pretended to walk with a limp. That way they would not recognize him. Because he didn't turn the light off when he left, they would assume he was still at home.

Once he could no longer be seen from the two housing blocks, he resumed his normal walking gait. He turned into an alleyway. There was a water tower at the end of it, though the pipes had yet to be installed.

There were no streetlights in the alleyway, but the moon had now risen and he walked softly in the moonlight, which shone as clearly as water on the paving stones. There were no footsteps behind him.

The alley did not extend far, and soon the water tower was standing before him. First he saw the sharp end of the tower, which stood quietly and ominously in the moonlight. Its full shape, which emerged when he left the alley, was chilling. It seemed like a huge, dark shadow, empty and formless.

All around was desolate, with a light shining only in a shack at the foot of the water tower. Quietly he made his way around the shack, and when he found the narrow iron ladder that was clamped to the water tower, he climbed it, rung by rung. The breeze grew stronger, and by the time he got to the top his clothes were puffed up by the wind and flapping as though torn. His hair blew across his face.

Now he had a bird's-eye view. In the moonlight the town looked gloomy and chilling, as if in a coma.

It's a plot, he thought.

16

Zhang Liang and the others swept in like a tide when he was still holed up in bed. He saw Yazhou and the other guys, plus a girl whom he had not seen before. He looked at them all in astonishment.

"How did you get in?" he asked.

They burst out laughing, as though they'd just heard a terrific joke. All of them except for the girl collapsed laughing into a chair, and the chair creaked as though it were laughing too.

"Who's she?" he asked.

They laughed even more loudly, and Zhang Liang stamped his foot on the floor in delight.

"Don't you recognize me?" The girl suddenly gathered in her laugh, and he was astounded that such a loud laugh could fade away so quickly.

"I'm Bai Xue," she said.

He was astonished, wondering how on earth he had failed to recognize her. Now, studying her carefully, he felt she did look a bit like Bai Xue. What's more, she was still wearing that red corduroy jacket, though it was no longer bright red but dark red.

"Time to get up," Bai Xue said.

So then Zhang Liang threw open his quilt. Four of them grabbed his arms and legs, picked him up, and threw him toward Bai Xue. He gave a cry of alarm, only to find that he was sitting very comfortably in a chair, while Bai Xue had sat down on the edge of the bed.

He didn't know what they were going to do next, so he put on an expectant air.

Zhang Liang tossed him some clothes, obviously wanting him to put them on. So he dressed. After that he sat back down in the chair and continued to wait.

"Let's go," Bai Xue said.

"Go where?" he asked.

She made no reply, but stood up and went outside. Zhang Liang and the rest came over and lifted him up, then pushed him toward the door.

"I haven't brushed my teeth yet," he said.

For no obvious reason Zhang Liang and the others burst out laughing once more.

So in just that way he was strong-armed into going downstairs. A lot of people were standing there, and it looked as though they'd been waiting a long time.

He saw how they pointed at him and made comments. As he walked on, he felt they were all falling in behind him. He wanted to make a run for it, but his arms were gripped by Zhang Liang and the others and he could not escape.

Then he was led out into the street, which he found was completely empty, devoid of people and activity. They marched him out into the middle of the street. Now, after vanishing for a while, Bai Xue appeared on the scene once more. She seemed to look at him pityingly, and then she strode off without saying a word.

Someone—he wasn't sure if it was Zhang Liang, or Zhu Qiao, or Hansheng, or perhaps Yazhou—said to him, "Look, who's there?"

He looked straight ahead, and there on the sidewalk not far away stood his father, smiling in his direction. Now he sud-

denly felt a truck was careening toward him from behind. But what was strange was that he heard the sound of a door being knocked on.

17

Later he slowly climbed down the iron ladder, and once more he stepped into the unlit alley. But now the windows on either side were illuminated by lamplight, and the light from inside brightened patches of the alleyway as well. Many of the windows were open, and voices talking inside could be heard clearly, although he couldn't make out what they were saying.

The alley was lined with houses—mostly old, single-story residences. As he walked, he would pause momentarily every time he passed an open window.

He was eager to know what the people inside were saying, because he felt they had to be talking about him. He knew that their meeting was over and his parents would be back home. So he felt a real need to stick his ear close to the windows. The reason he hesitated was that there were human figures visible through the windows, and the people inside were too close for comfort.

Finally he approached a suitable window. There were no figures in the window, but the voices inside were unusually clear. So he went over, hugging the wall, and gradually he could make out some of the words.

"Are you just about ready?"

"That's right."

"When do you start?"

But now he suddenly heard a noise behind him. "What are you doing?" It was as though someone was shouting in his ear. He spun around and knocked the man down with one punch. Then he began to run as fast as he could. The man gave a shout and behind him he heard a pounding of footsteps in hot pursuit, and at the same time many people stuck their heads out the windows.

He left the alleyway with this scenario in mind. He felt it was very realistic—if he were actually to put his ear up against a window, that's to say.

When he got home, his parents were already asleep. He put the light on. He reckoned it must now be quite late. Normally his parents went to bed at ten o'clock, and if he came home this late his father would deliver some woozy, bad-tempered words of censure. This time he didn't do that, but said calmly, "Hi there." He had not been sleeping.

He gave a curt response and headed off to his bedroom. Now he heard his mother say, "There's hot water in the thermos for you to wash your feet." Again he mumbled an acknowledgment, but once in his room he undressed and lay down in bed.

It was pitch-dark all around. After lying there for a while, he got up and went over to the window. He saw that many windows in the building opposite had now disappeared, and others were in the process of disappearing. His own block would be just the same, he thought. Now they could rest easy for a bit, for the next task would fall to his parents.

He went back to bed and lay down again. He had a hunch that something was about to happen, for they had obviously been preparing for a long time. His father had changed his attitude, and this signaled that they had noticed he was on guard. Quite possibly this would induce them to take action sooner than originally planned.

So now he needed urgently to exercise his imagination, to work out what action they might take against him the next day. Even though he had slept poorly the last two nights and was hard put to stay awake, he still did his utmost to avoid falling asleep.

Tomorrow morning, Zhang Liang and the gang, along with Bai Xue, would come over before he had gotten up. They would pretend to be in a boisterous mood, perhaps inviting him to go someplace or finding an excuse to stop him from going out. And then . . . He heard his breathing getting heavier.

18

The knocking was complex: in other words, there were several people pounding on the door at the same time. He was awake now, but everything that had just happened was vivid in his mind, even though he knew it was all a dream. Now the knocking on the door made him conscious of reality approaching.

He immediately decided that it was Zhang Liang and the gang, and Bai Xue, too. What was different from the dream was that they did not roll in like a tide. The door was blocking them.

Several of them at once were knocking on the door, and this showed they were annoyed.

But when he listened more carefully, it didn't sound as

though they were knocking on his door—it was as though they were knocking on the door opposite. He sat on the bed and heard the knocking growing louder and louder and sounding more and more like it was on the door opposite. So he put on his clothes and quietly went over to the door, and the knocking abruptly ceased.

He pondered for a moment, then opened the door decisively. Sure enough, Zhang Liang and the gang were standing outside. They roared with laughter at the sight of him. Then they rushed in all at once.

He was unmoved, feeling that their laughter and their boisterous entry corresponded to his dream of the night before.

Bai Xue, however, did not appear—it was just the four of them. But when they thronged inside, they did not pull the door to. Pretending to shut the door, he stuck his head out and looked around, but didn't see Bai Xue.

"Is it just the four of you?" he couldn't help asking.

"Isn't that enough?" Zhang Liang countered.

It is enough, he thought. Four against one is more than enough.

"Let's go," said Zhang Liang.

(If Bai Xue were present, it should be she who said that.)

"Go where?" he asked.

"You'll know when we get there."

"I haven't brushed my teeth yet," he said. As soon as he said this, he was stunned. Without intending to, he was repeating what he'd said in the dream.

"Let's go." So saying, Zhang Liang opened the door, while Zhu Qiao and Hansheng pinned his arms. (Just like in the dream.)

"We're going to take you somewhere that will really surprise you," Zhang Liang said when they got to the bottom of the stairs.

But there weren't many people watching, just three or four pedestrians on the move.

Zhu Qiao and Hansheng frog-marched him along as Zhang Liang and Yazhou led the way. He felt that Zhu Qiao and Hansheng were not using as much force as they had at the start.

All of a sudden, Zhang Liang shouted, "Once there was a mountain."

"On the mountain was a temple," Zhu Qiao continued.

Then it was Hansheng's turn. "In the temple were two monks."

A little pause, and Yazhou picked up the thread. "An old monk and a young monk."

Zhang Liang nudged him. "Your turn."

He looked at Zhang Liang in confusion.

"You say, 'The old one said to the young one.'"

He hesitated a moment, then said, "The old one said to the young one." They all laughed like crazy.

Zhang Liang picked up the thread again. "Once there was a mountain."

Zhu Qiao: "On the mountain was a temple."

Hansheng: "In the temple were two monks."

Yazhou: "An old monk and a young monk."

It was his turn now, but again he did not do his bit, because they had reached the main street. They were standing on the sidewalk.

"Hurry up," Zhang Liang said impatiently.

"The old one said to the young one," he said listlessly.

Zhang Liang was displeased. "Can't you say it a bit louder?"

Then, crying, "Once there was a mountain," he crossed the street. Zhu Qiao and Hansheng let go of him and followed Zhang Liang, shouting their lines as they went. Then Yazhou did the same.

Now it was his turn once more. He saw a truck slowly approaching to his left, and he knew that as soon as he got to the middle of the street it would come careening toward him.

19

What was this noise that kept chasing him and wouldn't give up? He'd been running so fast he was gasping for breath, but the noise was still on his tail and there was no way to shake it off.

In the end he huddled next to a utility pole and threw a glance back. The sound was approaching. It was his father.

His father was now standing right in front of him. "What's the matter with you?" he cried.

He looked at his father and made no reply. This is right, he thought. My father ought to make an appearance at this point. It simply came a bit later than in the dream.

"What's the matter with you?" his father asked again.

He felt sweat pouring out of all his pores. He was damp all over.

His father said nothing more and simply stared at him. Sweat was dripping down his forehead and blurring his vision. And so it looked as though his father were standing in the rain.

"Let's go home." His father's arm felt strong on his shoulders, and he had no choice but to follow.

"You're a grown-up now." He heard his father's voice circle around him, and it was as though his father was circling around him too. "You're a grown-up now." His father's voice continued to sound, but he could no longer make out the words.

As they walked back along the street, he noticed that his father's footsteps were poorly coordinated with his own. His father's tone, in contrast, was quite cordial, though this cordiality was bogus.

Later—he hadn't registered just where they'd got to—his father suddenly made some remark or other and left him.

Now for the first time he scanned the surroundings attentively. He saw that his father was crossing the street to where someone else was standing. He felt that this person looked rather familiar, but he couldn't immediately think who it was. The man threw him a smile. His father stopped in front of him, and the two of them began to converse.

He stood where he was, as if waiting for his father to come back, or perhaps wondering whether he should leave. Then he heard something fall out of the sky and hit the ground nearby. When he turned his head, there was a brick lying there. He gave a start, realizing now that he was standing directly beneath a building. Looking up, he saw someone perched on the scaffolding above. It was a middle-aged man, a lot like the one who had leaned against the plane tree. He felt that any minute a brick would come hurtling toward his head.

20

The man was leaning against a plane tree, right next to the street. Although he wasn't smoking a cigarette, he was definitely the man he was looking for.

He remembered, now, that this was the place where Bai Xue first signaled to him. At that time he was still completely in the dark; at that time he was in a buoyant mood. He had just made his escape from that creepy building, and he didn't know why he ended up here.

When he came to a stop about ten meters away, the man took notice. He said to himself: That's right, he's the one.

As he slowly approached the man, the man's expression grew more and more wary, and the hand he'd kept in his pocket slowly began to emerge. And the people walking in the street slowed their pace to watch him—he knew they might rush him at any time.

He went up to the man. The man was rubbing his hands in front of his chest as though ready to throw a punch at any moment, and his legs were tensed.

But he stuck his hands in his pant pockets and said with composure, "I'd like to have a word with you."

The man perceptibly relaxed and seemed to smile. "You're looking for me?" he asked.

"That's right," he said.

The man looked toward the street, as though to deliver a signal. "Go ahead."

"Not here," he said. "I want to talk to you alone."

The man looked hesitant. He did not want to leave the plane tree, meaning he did not want to leave those accomplices of his who were pretending to be pedestrians.

He gave a smirk. "You don't dare?"

The man laughed loudly. "Let's go," he said.

So he began to lead the way, the other man following close behind. He walked with a measured pace, so that he could repel at any time a sneak attack. Now he heard a disorderly medley of footsteps behind him, which meant there were now several people following him. He did not look back. "It has to be just you and me," he said.

The man made no reply and the footsteps behind him did not diminish in number.

"If you don't have the guts, just leave."

Again the man laughed.

He continued forward, but stopped for a moment when he got to the entrance to an alley. Only when he saw there was nobody in the alley did he enter. Now the steps behind him dwindled.

He couldn't help but smile as he proceeded to the deepest section of the alley. The man was close behind. He knew he could not afford to look back now, for if he did, that would put the man on guard and he would keep a few steps back. So he walked on as though at ease, while mentally calculating the distance between them. It seemed a little too far. So he unobtrusively slowed his pace, and the man did not notice.

Now he felt things were just about right, so he swiftly crouched, putting his weight on his left leg and at the same

*time stamping backward with his right foot. He heard a
scream, and then the sounds of a stumble and fall. He looked
back to find the man, his face pale, sitting on the ground and
clutching his stomach in pain.*

*He took a step forward and aimed another kick, this time at
the man's face. The man groaned and fell to the ground.*

"Tell me, what were you trying to do?" he asked.

*"I wanted Zhang Liang and the others to steer you into the
middle of the street and have a truck hit you."*

"I know that," he said.

*"If that didn't work, I was going to have your father lead
you under that building and let a brick fall on your head."*

"And then?" he asked.

The man was still leaning against the plane tree. Now he
stuck his hand into his chest pocket and pulled out a cigarette
and lit it.

It's definitely him, he thought. But he lacked the determination to confront him. He felt that if the two of them did
face off, the outcome would be the opposite of what he had
just imagined. The one left moaning on the ground, in other
words, would be he himself. This man was heavily built, after
all, and he was so weak and scrawny.

The man no longer looked so distracted; his gaze was distinctly hostile.

He suddenly realized he had been standing here too long.

21

"Do you know something?" Bai Xue said.

He had no idea how he had arrived at Bai Xue's house. He recalled that one day a couple of years earlier he had seen her glide out of this door, just as she glided out now.

Bai Xue clearly had been startled to see him.

And he noticed that she was a bit embarrassed—window dressing, of course.

Bai Xue's bedroom was stylish, but not as tidy as Hansheng's. When he sat down on a chair, Bai Xue blushed a little, but it was natural for her to blush—in the final analysis she was different from them, he thought.

It was then that Bai Xue said, "Do you know something?"

She planned to tell him everything directly—now it was he who was astonished.

"Yesterday I ran into Zhang Liang in the street. . . ."

Sure enough, she was going to spill the beans.

"He suddenly called my name." No sooner had her normal coloring returned than she again reddened. "We never talked to each other in school, so I was flabbergasted. . . ."

He began to be perplexed, not knowing what Bai Xue would go on to say.

"Zhang Liang said that you all would come over to my house today—you, Zhu Qiao, Hansheng, and Yazhou. He said it was your idea. They were here this morning."

Now he understood. Bai Xue was trying to cover up for the

activities of Zhang Liang and the others that morning. She was more devious than he had imagined.

"Why didn't you come with them?" she asked.

He didn't know what to say and could only look at her mournfully. He now saw a dramatic change in Bai Xue's expression: she looked rather stunned.

She's learned how to perform, he said to himself.

A long time seemed to pass, and he saw that Bai Xue was at a loss. It seemed she didn't know where to put her hands.

"Do you remember what happened the other day?" he said. "I saw you as I was walking down the street. You signaled to me."

Bai Xue turned bright red. She sputtered a reply: "I thought you were smiling at me, so I smiled too—how did you get the idea it was a signal?"

So, she's determined to playact, he thought. But he continued undeterred. "Do you remember there was a middle-aged man close by?"

She shook her head.

"He was leaning against a plane tree," he said, to jog her memory.

But still she shook her head.

"So, what was it you were signaling?" He couldn't help losing patience.

She gazed at him as if dumbfounded. "What makes you think it was a signal?" she said uneasily.

He ignored this. "From then on I realized I was being watched."

Now she assumed an air of utter bewilderment. "Who's watching you?" she asked.

"Everyone."

It looked as though she wanted to laugh but decided against it, given how serious he was. She did venture a comment, however. "You love to joke."

"Cut out the playacting!" he cried.

She gave a start and looked at him fearfully.

"Tell me this: Why are they watching me, and what are they going to do next?"

She shook her head. "I don't know what you mean."

He could only sigh with disappointment, for he could see she would tell him nothing. She was no longer the Bai Xue in a yellow blouse. Now she was wearing a dark red jacket. He was astonished to find he had only just noticed.

He stood up and left Bai Xue's bedroom; he realized the kitchen was on the right. When he entered the kitchen, he saw a knife sitting there. He picked it up and tested its sharpness: it would do. He went back into Bai Xue's room, knife in hand. Now he saw her jump to her feet in alarm and retreat to the corner of the room. As he stepped forward, he heard her give a cry of panic. Then he pressed the knife against her throat and she trembled with fear.

Bai Xue stood up, and so did he. But he was unsure whether to go to the kitchen and get the knife.

He saw Bai Xue go over to the calendar on the wall. She tore off a page, then looked at him over her shoulder. "Tomorrow is April Third."

He was still hesitating over whether or not to go to the kitchen.

"How about you guess?" Bai Xue said. "What's going to happen tomorrow?"

He was startled. What would happen on April Third? April

Third? He remembered now. His mother had mentioned this, and so had his father.

He understood that Bai Xue was dropping a hint; she could not say things in so many words, because she had worries of her own. He felt he ought to leave: further delay might make things tricky for her.

As he came out of the bedroom, he realized the kitchen was not on the right but on the left.

22

He had never known that the long moan of a train horn could raise his spirits so high.

At this time he had found himself a hiding place on the fourth floor of a building; he was sitting beneath the window. He'd slipped in at dusk, seen by no one. The building still lacked a staircase, and so he had climbed up the scaffolding. He watched as the night sky grew ever darker and listened as the sounds in the street faded into the distance. In the end even the man selling wonton down below had packed up his stall and gone home. A bit like how smoke dissipates in the air, the noises of human beings dissipated too. It was only his own breath that murmured quietly, as though he were talking to himself.

He did not know what to do now, just as he did not know what time it was. But tomorrow—April Third—something was going to happen. He was very clear on that score. He didn't know what he should do about it, however.

He heard a train horn. This gave him an inspiration, and

he stood up. When he stood up, the first thing he saw was a bridge, a bridge that just lay there as though dead. Then he noticed the little river, flowing ominously. Its waves glittered, like countless blinking eyes watching him. He laughed coldly.

Then he climbed out the window and slid down the scaffolding, which creaked like a door.

He followed the shadow-darkened street toward the railroad line. He did not hear his own footsteps; their sound seemed to be have been soaked up by the ground. He felt he was floating along like a breeze.

Before long he was standing on the tracks, which gleamed in the moonlight. On the platform of the little station nearby a single dim, yellow light was shining, and he saw nobody about. Opposite him, a dim light was also shining in the lineman's little cabin. There had to be someone inside, perhaps already dozing off. He looked again at the railroad tracks, still bathed in moonlight.

Now he heard a sound like a wave surging. It came closer and closer and slowly expanded. He felt the noise blow his hair, and then he saw a sharp, bright light pointing his way, and then the light came sweeping toward him, only to be blocked by his body.

The train was beginning to slow down. It was a freight train, and it came to a stop next to him. Human figures appeared on the platform. He rushed forward and grabbed the metal ladder attached to one of the cars. It was even narrower than the ladder of the water tower. He climbed up and into the car, only to find it was loaded with coal. So he lay down on the pile of coal, and at the same time heard people talking. Their voices seemed to be blown into pieces by the wind, so that when they reached his ears they were just scraps.

Perhaps they had turned out in full force, it occurred to him. He had not gone home all day and his parents would surely suspect he would try to make a run for it. So they would have informed the neighbors opposite, and soon all the lights in that dark housing block would come on, and then all the lights in town. Even without closing his eyes he could imagine the clamor and excitement as they launched their search.

Now he heard the footsteps of someone walking past, so he quickly turned and lay on his stomach as flat as he could. Then came the noise of wheels revolving over the rails, a crisp sound that spread in all directions like lamplight. The footsteps faded into the distance.

Suddenly he heard the train emit a ponderous sound and at the same time he felt his body shake. Almost immediately he saw the station slowly moving, and a breeze began to move with it. As the wind blew more strongly, the noise of the wheels on the rails grew smoother.

He sat up straight on the coal heap. He saw the station tossed into the distance and the whole town along with it. The town receded farther and farther, and soon he could see nothing at all; behind him there was only a pale darkness. Tomorrow would be April Third, he thought. He began to imagine how disconsolate and demoralized they would all be. Without doubt his parents would be punished for failing in their duty. The realization that he had completely shattered their plot filled him with triumph.

Then he turned his head and let the wind blow on his face. Ahead there also lay a pale darkness, and there too he could see nothing at all. But he knew he was now moving farther and farther away from the plot. They would never be able to find him. Tomorrow and forever, the very mention of his name would reduce them to speechless despair.

He thought of a boy he had known when he was younger, and the harmonica that the boy used to play. Every evening he would head over to the house where he lived, and the boy would lean over the windowsill and play that harmonica of his. Later the boy died of hepatitis at the age of eighteen, and the harmonica died then, too.

Death Chronicle

It had not actually been my plan at all to head off in that direction, which only goes to show that things were predestined to happen the way they did. I had arrived at a fork in the road and noticed a sign pointing to the right: QIANMU MARSH, 60 KILOMETERS. So my truck turned right, and that's what got me into trouble. It was the second time I ended up in that kind of mess.

The first time was in the hills of southern Anhui—that was over ten years ago. I was steering my Liberation truck—not the Yellow River I'm driving now—down a narrow, winding mountain road, when I knocked a boy into the reservoir way down below. I really couldn't help it. My truck was trundling downhill at a pretty good clip, and after making it round the seventh hairpin bend I suddenly realized there was a kid in front of me—just three or four meters ahead—going downhill on a bicycle. I had no time to brake—all I could do was swerve to one side or the other. But if I swerved to the left, I would smash into the mountainside and my Liberation would explode, would erupt in flames, and I would be reduced to ashes long before the crematorium had time to get in on the act. And if I swerved to the right, my Liberation would tip straight into the reservoir. The thud of such a heavy load hitting the water would surely be terrifying, and the wave it

threw up would be huge, and there could be no other outcome but me being drowned. In short, I had no choice—the
only option was to knock the boy into the reservoir. The boy
turned his head in alarm and looked at me. He had dark, glittering eyes, which I still remembered long after the event—
often, when I shut my eyes, those black, bright eyes of his
would leap out at me. No sooner did he throw me that glance
than his body was flung into the air sideways, the wind inflat-
ing his clothes—he was wearing an adult-size pair of overalls.
He gave a shout—"Dad!"—and that was all. It was a loud,
piercing cry, which I heard twice—the second time was when
it echoed off the cliff face. The echo seemed insubstantial, as
though blown my way from some far-off cloud. I didn't stop
the truck, for I was scared stupid. It was only when the truck
got to the foot of the slope and raced onto the broad, flat highway below that I was able to pull myself together and marvel
that I hadn't fallen off the mountain. *I* might have been stupid, but I guess my hands were not—I had years of driving
experience, after all.

Nobody knows what happened, and I've had no reason to
talk about it. I suppose that boy must have been the son of a
forestry worker. I wonder if the man wept when he fished his
son out of the reservoir later. Maybe he had a whole bunch of
sons, though, so it probably didn't make much difference to
him if one of them snuffed it. Those mountain folk have lots
of kids. I reckon the boy must have been fourteen or fifteen
years old. It can't have been easy for the dad to raise him to
that age, mind you—it must have cost him a real packet, after
all. So it was too bad the kid died. The bicycle was wrecked as
well, to make it worse.

I'd actually forgotten about this, forgotten about it completely. But my own son started growing up, and once he was fifteen he began to nag me about wanting to learn how to ride a bicycle, so I taught him. He's a smart little fellow, and in no time at all he could ride around in a circle without needing me to hold him steady. Seeing the ecstatic look on his face, I felt ecstatic too. Fifteen years ago, when he was just born, he really scared the shit out of me. He didn't look human—he looked more like a toy you buy in the store. In those days he would just lie in his cradle kicking his feet about, pissing here, shitting there, and farting loudly as well—what smelly farts those were! But in no time at all he's already grown so big, riding around on a bike so full of confidence. I've done all I can in life—from now on it's all up to my son. He's a fine boy, and he puts me in a good light—his teachers are always praising him. In the past when I took the truck out on a job, I'd always be thinking of the wife, but once I had a son I thought only of him and stopped thinking about her. Then, as my son was gaily riding his bike around, I don't know why, but some little devil got me thinking about that boy who fell into the reservoir over ten years ago. Seen from behind, my son on his bike looked just like that kid—particularly with that head of black hair, he was practically the spitting image. And so that pair of overalls came into my mind. The worst thing was that my son ran right into a tree that day and cried "Dad!" in great alarm. His shout made me shiver inside, and the image of the boy soaring through the air and plummeting into the water suddenly flashed into my mind. What was weird was that my son's cry, though it came from just a few meters away, to my ears sounded very distant, like the echo I heard in the mountains. That boy's cry of panic, forgotten for so many years, issued for a second time from the mouth of my son, and for a moment

I had the strange sensation that it was my own child I had knocked into the reservoir. After that, I would sometimes get sad for no reason. I never told anyone about what happened, and even my wife doesn't know. It continued to bother me that the boy kept coming back to mind long after the event. But things might get better in a few years' time, I thought: once my son was eighteen, maybe I would no longer see in him the shadow of that boy on the bicycle.

Just like with the first incident, I had not the slightest inkling that the second was going to happen. I remember that the weather was perfect; the sky was so blue I didn't dare look at it. I was in an ordinary mood, neither good nor bad. I rolled down both windows and unbuttoned my shirt; the breeze felt great. My Yellow River truck made a noise like a cow's moo—a solid, reassuring sound. I sped along the asphalt highway as though on a carefree outing; I was going sixty kilometers an hour. The road spun under my wheels like cloth on a dyeing machine. My wife works in the dyeing factory, that's why I thought of it. But I had only gone thirty kilometers when the asphalt surface came to an end and a potholed road began. It could almost have been carpet bombed, that's how bad it was, and sitting in the truck I felt as though I were riding bareback on a horse. I hated all the shaking and the sensation that at any moment I might be bounced out of my seat. The stuff inside my belly was heaving back and forth as well. So I stopped the truck. A Liberation came rumbling up from the other direction, and when it got close I hailed the driver and asked, "What kind of road is this?"

"First time here?" he asked.

I nodded.

"No wonder you're surprised," he said. "It's called 'the Boneshaker.'"

There in the cabin I kept bouncing around like a jumping flea, so how could I not feel dizzy? Later I became vaguely aware that the sea was off to my right, a huge expanse of muddy water in an endless roiling tide, and the roar of the tide made my belly seethe: I felt there was a muddy sea inside me too. I stuck my head out the window and barfed like crazy, and what I barfed was a muddy chowder, sure enough. I barfed until my eyes were streaming and my legs were shivering and my midriff was practically in spasms. If I kept on barfing like that, I thought to myself, I'd be barfing up my whole belly, so I clapped a hand over my mouth.

Now I could see a broad asphalt road not far ahead, and before long my truck would make it off this bone-shaking surface and race onto the level highway. By now I had vomited everything up, which was a big relief, except that it left me feeling feeble and faint. I continued to be tossed around in my seat, but I no longer felt queasy, and even began to unwind a little bit. And when I saw how the asphalt road was getting closer and closer, my spirits began to pick up. But where I really got screwed was when I'd made it down onto the highway and my stomach started acting up again. I knew it had nothing to act up *with*, since I had already thrown up everything I had inside, but all the empty retching was even more unpleasant. My mouth fell open because I just couldn't keep it shut, and out of my throat emerged a bizarre series of sounds, as though an inch-long fish bone had got stuck somewhere. Again I felt like throwing up, but all I could produce was noise, along with some smelly air. Tears dripped from my eyes once more and my legs no longer just shivered but shook uncontrollably, and I could practically hear my kidneys groaning with all the cramps in my midriff. A sour drool dribbled from the corners of my mouth and slithered down my chin, onto my neck and chest, and then down to my midriff, where all those cramps were going on. The stuff was cold and sticky and I wanted to rub it off with my hand, but I didn't have the strength to do even that.

Just at that moment I saw a human figure flit into view ahead of me and I heard a heavy thump. Weak and distracted though I was, I knew something bad had happened. Somehow my energy revived and I was able to stamp on the brakes hard enough that the truck ground to a halt. But then I just couldn't get the door open—my hand was trembling too much. A bus drove past, its passengers staring out the windows. I thought they were sure to have seen something, so I gave up on the door and sat numbly in my seat, waiting as the bus stopped in the distance, waiting for people to come running over. But a long time passed and none of the passengers appeared. A few country women did walk in my direction, their eyes glued to the truck, and I thought that this time somebody was bound to see something, for sure they would shout and make a commotion, but they walked right past as though nothing had happened. So I began to develop doubts, to wonder whether my eyes had been playing tricks on me. Then somehow the door opened without any difficulty and I jumped out to look at the front of the truck: there was nothing unusual there. I went around the truck twice and still could see nothing wrong. So I began to relax, thinking I must have been imagining things. I gave a long sigh of relief, which drained me of energy once more.

If I hadn't seen bloodstains on the wheels, if I had just nipped back into the cabin and carried on driving, perhaps nothing would have happened. But I did see them. Not only that, I put my hand on the stains and found the blood was still wet. Then I knew for sure I had not been imagining things. So I got down on the ground and took a peek underneath the truck. I saw a girl lying curled up there.

I stood up and looked around vacantly, waiting for someone to come and investigate. It was summer, in the middle of the day, and the sun was beating down lazily and everywhere seemed to be smoking. There was a little river on the left, but it didn't seem to be moving—it looked more like it was covered in moss. A concrete bridge spanned the river, with a railing on one side. A muddy road with tall grass growing on both sides stretched off into the distance, where a few houses lay; I thought I spotted some people there too. I waited, but nobody showed up.

I stared at the bloodstains on the wheels a bit more, and after looking at them a long time I realized there really weren't that many, just a few drops here and there. So I bent down and grabbed a handful of dirt and began to slowly mop up those drops of blood, and when I'd got through half the job I stopped to light a cigarette; then I went on mopping. Only when I had rubbed the blood away did I seem to wake from my daze. Get out of here, I told myself. Stop hanging around! I got in the truck right away. But just when I'd slammed the door and started the engine, suddenly I saw in front of me a fourteen- or fifteen-year-old boy, wearing a large pair of overalls and riding a bicycle. The boy I'd knocked into the reservoir over ten years ago somehow reappeared at this very moment. It was all ordained by fate. Even though that scene simply flickered for a second and then abruptly disappeared, there was no way I could just drive away.

I got back down and dragged the girl out from underneath the truck. Her forehead was horribly mangled. But blood was still flowing from her wound, and though her breath was faint, at least she was breathing. Her eyes were staring—dark, bright eyes just like that pair of eyes from a dozen years earlier. I took her in my arms and carried her across the concrete bridge with the single railing, until I made it to the dirt road. Her soft body was burning hot and her long black hair hung loose, resting on my arms like a willow frond. I felt a piercing sadness, as though the injured child was my own. As I held her in my arms, she rested her head on my chest, making it look all the more like she was my own child. I walked for a long time with her nestled in my arms like that, and the houses I had glimpsed from the highway grew bigger, though the human figures I had seen earlier were now absent. Suddenly a quiver of excitement surged up inside me, for I had a vague sense that I was doing something noble. My thoughts returned to the scene of the accident a dozen years earlier, and it was as though I hadn't done a hit-and-run but had dived into the reservoir and saved the boy, as though the child I carried in my arms was the boy in the oversize overalls. The black hair dangling over my arm simply showed how long the boy's hair had grown during the intervening years.

As I drew nearer to the houses, I realized there were still more houses beyond them. A large tree blocked my path and in its shade an old woman sat topless, her dried-up breasts hanging all the way to her waist. She was watching me, and when I went over and asked where I would find a hospital, she saw the girl in my arms and gave a scream. "You're in for it now!" she cried.

That cry alerted me that I had made a big mistake by not making good my escape. But now it was too late. I looked down at the girl to find that blood was no longer dripping from her forehead and her black hair was no longer waving free, for blood had glued it together. Her body seemed to be losing its warmth—though actually it was my own heart cooling down. Again I asked the old woman directions to a hospital, and again she answered with a shriek. She was frightened dumb by the awful sight, I thought, and I knew I would get no answer from her if I asked again. So I skirted the tree and proceeded. But the old woman followed me, shouting over and over, "You're in for it now!" Soon she had rushed ahead, shrieking incessantly with a cry as grating as the sound of breaking glass. I saw a few piglets scurry past, and then several other old women appeared. Coming up to me, they took one look and then they too cried, "You're in for it now!" So I followed along behind the old women as they wailed, though I was now utterly confused, unsure what was the point of my going in this direction. Before long, there was a big crowd of people on all sides, and my ears were buzzing with a chaotic hubbub of voices. I couldn't absorb anything they were saying—all I noticed was that there were men and women, young and old. Only now did it dawn on me that I was in a village—how could I expect to find a hospital in a village? Suddenly it all seemed ridiculous. The road ahead was crammed, so I turned around, only to find that way was blocked by just as dense a throng.

I realized I was standing by a small drying ground, adjacent to a two-story house—newly built, by the look of it. A tall, burly fellow emerged from inside and snatched the girl away from me; trailing behind him were a woman and a boy in his teens. Then they all scuttled inside the house.

It happened so quickly I was a bit dazed. But now that I was relieved of my burden, I felt I ought to get back to the truck. Just as I turned around and made ready to leave, someone came up to me and punched me in the jaw. The impact made a dull sound, like a fist hitting a sofa. No sooner did I turn back toward the house than the teenage boy came racing out, waving aloft a shiny sickle. As he lunged toward me, the flailing sickle swept down and struck me in the midriff, slicing through my skin as though it were paper and severing my gut. As he yanked on the sickle, it carved through my buttocks and cut such a long, deep tear that my intestines began to slither right out. Before I could clamp my hand on the wound, the woman flailed at me with a hoe. I managed to duck, but the blade of her weapon hacked into my shoulder like an axe cutting wood, and my shoulder blade snapped with a loud thunk, like a door flung open. The burly fellow was the last one to rush at me; he was brandishing an iron rake. Even as the hoe still dangled from my shoulder, the four teeth of the rake had already plunged into my chest. The middle teeth severed my pulmonary artery and aorta and blood gushed out with a whoosh, as though someone were dumping a basinful of foot-wash water. The outer teeth punctured my two lungs, and one of them pierced my heart. When the man tugged on the rake, my lungs came flopping out and I collapsed on the ground. I lay faceup as my blood spilled in all directions, like the spreading roots of an ancient tree. I died.

In Memory of Miss Willow Yang

1

For a long time now I have led a life of self-indulgent ease. I live in a place called Smoke, in a one-room cottage overlooking the river, and though the cottage is no more than a mundane rectangle, its boxy shape evokes the simple lines and uncluttered routine of my life.

As I roam around the town, I delight in the sound of my footsteps, a music that only a stranger's heels can make. Despite the length of my stay here, I have successfully managed to defend the purity of my footsteps, which have never been corrupted no matter how worldly the clamor of the street.

I refuse all dangerous associations. The smiles that I encounter alarm me with their eagerness for contact, and I rebuff them at once, for I can easily detect the sinister intentions they are so bent on concealing. Each wearer of a smile is aiming to come into my life and occupy it. He'll clap a coarse hand on my shoulder and force me to open my door; he'll lie down on my bed as if it were his, and casually alter the position of my chair. When leaving, he'll give three successive sneezes that forever lay claim to my living space, and even if I light mosquito coils everywhere it'll be impossible to smoke them all away. Then, before I know it, he'll bring along a pack of cronies who reek of vulgar kitchen stench. Though they may not sneeze, their mouths will be full of bacteria and with their loud talk and raucous laughter they'll bathe my room in germs. At that point I won't just feel my life has been hijacked; I'll feel I've been stabbed in the back as well.

I prefer to schedule my excursions at nighttime, not because I doubt my resolve to spurn all friendly overtures, but because the dim light gives me a reassuring sense that I have ventured beyond the reach of common people. After a careful study of the windows in the houses nearby, I notice that every single window has its curtains drawn, and I find comfort in the knowledge that the curtains separate me from others. But danger still lurks, for even stringent isolation cannot protect me fully. Often when I enter the narrow streets of the neighborhood, I feel I am marching down the corridor of a hepatitis ward, and I can never afford to lower my guard.

It's at night that I observe the curtains. At that hour, the streetlights behind me endow them with an impenetrable mystique, and when the breeze catches a curtain and ruffles its folds, its pattern will stir bewitchingly. This makes me think of the river that runs past my lodging and how its bends and eddies have inspired the countless scenes of fluttering snow-flakes that punctuate my dreams. More often, however, the curtains are motionless, allowing me time to take full measure of their brightness. Even if changes in lighting and the curtains' rich colors may complicate my observations, once I adjusted for those variables I found that their radiance is just like the glance of a snake that has coiled itself in the middle of a pitch-dark street. Ever since I gained that insight, each time I enter one of these residential streets I feel as though I'm being watched by a thousand pairs of beady eyes.

It was at a much later date, on May 8, 1988, that a young woman walked toward me. Her role was to make my life develop a flaw, or enable it to become more perfect. To put it another way, her arrival would have such effects as these: I would wake up one morning to find that the room had acquired an extra bed, or find that my own bed had vanished into thin air.

2

The outlander is actually no stranger to me. He comes from a place where the grass grows tall—simply the sight of his veins told me that. The first time we met was in the middle of a summer's day, and he was naked to the waist in the sweltering heat. His skin made me think of a tree trunk just stripped of its bark, and his veins spread as luxuriantly as green grass.

I find it hard to remember exactly when that was, but it seems a long time ago. If I think back carefully, I can recall the color of the sky and the trill of the cicadas in the trees. The outlander was sitting under the arch of a bridge. I was impressed that he had chosen such an original spot to seek refuge from the heat.

The outlander is the kind of person who puts me at ease from the start: I found his serenity appealing. Even when I was still a good ten meters from him, I knew that he was not the sort who would knock on my door, sleep on my bed, or harbor designs on my chair. I walked toward him fully aware that some kind of verbal exchange would ensue, but knowing that a conversation with him would take a very different form from that with a woman who's washing vegetables or a man lighting a coal stove. So when he smiled at me, a reciprocal smile appeared on my face and we began to talk.

Out of caution, initially I stood outside the arch. But as he spoke, he indicated through a series of gestures that he welcomed me to come inside, so I joined him under the arch. He promptly picked up several sheets of paper from the ground and scrawled lines all over them, lines that looked a lot like his gestures. I sat down in the spot where the papers had lain, knowing this would please him. Now his smile was just an arm's length away. Of all the smiles I had encountered in Smoke, his was the only one that promised me safety.

He talked in a steady tone that seemed much like the river's leisurely roll as it flowed beneath the bridge, and so from the very start I felt at home with his voice. Given that the circumstances under which we became acquainted were neither dramatic nor remarkable, his level tone seemed highly appropriate. He now dispensed with his hand gestures, so that I would pay full attention to what he was saying. He told me a story about time bombs that dated back to a distant war.

In early 1949, Tang Enbo, commander of the Nationalist garrison in Shanghai, decided to abandon Suzhou and Hangzhou to the advancing Communist troops and concentrate his forces for the defense of Shanghai. Nationalist soldiers of a company stationed in the little town of Smoke withdrew from their positions overnight. But before they did so, an officer named Tan Liang directed sappers to bury ten time bombs. Tan Liang was a mathematics graduate of Tongji University.

That night, under a sky strewn with stars, he buried the bombs in an intricate geometric pattern.

Tan Liang was the last Nationalist officer to evacuate from Smoke, and as he left the little town and gazed back to survey it one last time, it looked as quiet as a bamboo grove in the starlight. At that moment he perhaps already had a premonition that decades later he would stand once more in that spot, a premonition that would become reality on September 3, 1988.

Although Tan Liang joined his company in their deployment to Shanghai, he did not end up among the long columns of soldiers who surrendered to the Communist forces. He had left Shanghai prior to this time, along with his team of sappers, who had relocated to the offshore island of Zhoushan. With the fall of Zhoushan, Tan Liang disappeared from view. Among the multitude of Nationalist officers and soldiers who fled to Taiwan, three had been soldiers in Tan Liang's sapper team. They thought it almost certain that he had drowned en route, because they had seen with their own eyes how the flimsy sailing boat in which he was attempting the passage was smashed to pieces in a storm.

On September 2, 1988, an old fisherman named Shen Liang arrived at Dinghai, Zhoushan's main port, and at five o'clock that afternoon he boarded a ferry bound for Shanghai. That night he lay in an upper bunk and endured a night of incessant rocking and tossing that seemed to last for decades. Early the next morning the ferry docked at Pier 16, on the waterfront near the bund. Shen Liang came ashore amid a throng of passengers and took a city bus to the long-distance bus terminal in Xujiahui, where he bought a ticket for the 7:30 a.m. departure to the little town of Smoke.

On the morning of September 3, the seat next to him was occupied by a young man from a distant province. He had spent a month being treated for an eye condition in a Shanghai hospital, and after discharge he had chosen not to go home directly, but to make a detour to Smoke. During the journey, Shen Liang told him how, decades earlier, a Nationalist officer named Tan Liang had directed sappers to plant ten bombs in the town where they were now heading.

3

"Ten years ago," the outlander said.

Although his voice remained steady, I felt a change, as though the water under the bridge had stopped flowing downriver and was now moving in the opposite direction. The outlander's expression conveyed clearly that he had begun to tell a different story.

"Ten years ago," he went on. "That's to say, May eighth, 1988."

I felt he must have made a mistake, because it was not yet May 8, 1988. So I corrected him: "You mean 1978."

"No"—he waved his hand in disagreement—"1988. If it had been 1978," he explained, "that would be twenty years ago."

4

Ten years ago, that's to say on May 8, 1988, something unexpected happened in the outlander's personal life. It was this event that led to his arrival several months later in the little town of Smoke.

Not long after May 8, his eyes began to water constantly, and at the same time his vision gradually grew cloudy. He alone was aware of these changes, for he told nobody, not even closest family. He vaguely felt that the deterioration in his sight was related to what had happened on May 8, but it was such a private matter that he was disinclined to let others know. He simply felt things slipping out of his control, as the scenes around him grew more and more murky and indistinct.

His condition continued to worsen, to the point that one day, when his father was sitting out on the balcony reading a newspaper, the outlander grabbed him by the collar, mistaking him for a down blanket. Within a couple of days almost all his acquaintances were aware that his eyes were traveling down a road toward utter darkness. And so he was admitted to a local hospital.

From that day on, he no longer took responsibility for his own body and gave others license to exert authority over it. But constantly in his mind he was mulling over his private affairs; only he knew why his eyes were tending toward blurriness. He was vaguely aware of traveling on a bus, and then a train. The train arrived at a terminal, and he was wheeled into a Shanghai hospital.

Less than two weeks after his admission to the hospital, on August 14, 1988, a traffic accident occurred on a street in Hongkou district in north Shanghai: a young woman from out of town was hit by a speeding Liberation truck. She was rushed to the hospital where the outlander was being treated, but she died on the operating table four hours later. Shortly before her death, knowing there was no way to save her, the chief surgeon raised the issue of organ donation with her father, who was sitting helplessly on a bench outside. The man was utterly distraught because of the tragedy that so suddenly had befallen his daughter. Understanding nothing, he agreed to everything that was proposed.

After the extraction of the young woman's eye tissue, three surgeons performed a corneal transplant. On the morning of September 1, 1988, the gauze was removed from the outlander's eyes. He felt as though a folding fan waved for a moment in front of him, and then the darkness fell away. Now he could see that a man was standing by his bedside—or, to be more precise, he could see that his father was.

The outlander spent another two nights in the ward and was formally discharged on September 3. That morning he arrived in the long-haul bus station in Xujiahui and boarded a bus bound for Smoke. His father saw him off at the bus station, then left to take a train back home.

The outlander had only just learned about the town called Smoke. He wanted to visit the family home of Willow Yang, who had died in a traffic accident at the age of seventeen. According to a nurse, it was her corneas that had been donated to him. He had obtained Willow Yang's address from the hospital cashier: she lived in Smoke, at 26 Carpenter Square Alley.

Shanghai is connected to Smoke by an asphalt highway, and on that overcast autumn morning the outlander, now in the third day since he regained his sight, gazed out the window at the drab scenery. His neighbor was an old man; though neatly dressed, he exuded a somewhat fishy odor. His eyes were closed for much of the journey, and he opened them only when the bus reached Jinshan. It was in the last few kilometers that the old man began to talk. He told the outlander that his name was Shen Liang and he was a native of Zhoushan, emphasizing particularly this latter point: "It's the first time in my life I've left Zhoushan."

The conversation did not stop there, but involved a war of decades earlier. In fact, the whole conversation consisted simply of the old man talking and the outlander listening as he looked out the window.

As though reminiscing about old times in the comfort of his own home, the old man related the story of a Nationalist officer named Tan Liang and the ten time bombs. As they neared their destination, the old man had reached the point in early 1949 when Tan Liang took one last look at Smoke and found the little town as quiet as a bamboo grove.

As the bus entered the town, the overcast skies turned dark and chaotic and the old man's speech came to a sudden halt; his eyes were like those of a dead fish. He said nothing more. The matter of Tan Liang coming to grief in a shipwreck emerged several days later, when the old man and the outlander met and conversed a second time, on the concrete bridge. It was then that the outlander learned of Tan Liang's death at sea.

The bus drove into Smoke's bus station. The outlander and Shen Liang were the last two passengers to leave the station. Several people were waiting outside to meet travelers coming off the bus. Two men stood smoking, and a woman greeted a man on a bicycle. The outlander and Shen Liang walked side by side for some twenty meters, and then Shen Liang came to a stop and surveyed the town that now lay before him in the midday light. The outlander kept on going, and as he walked, something prompted him to recall the last scene that Shen Liang had described to him on the bus—how, when leaving Smoke in early 1949, Tan Liang had looked back in the moonlight and found the little town as quiet as a bamboo grove.

The outlander continued on. Noticing a young woman by the side of the road who seemed to be waiting for someone, he asked for directions to a hotel. She pointed off into the distance.

As he walked farther, the trees lining the two sides of the concrete road looked lifeless under the leaden sky, as though they'd been covered in dust. But the walls of the houses— even old walls with faded whitewash—were gleaming brightly.

Later he reached a concrete bridge and came to a stop. Several thousand laborers were dredging the river below. He strolled onto the bridge and stood to watch, and so he came to witness the unearthing of an explosive device. At that moment a story about time bombs filled his mind, while an address on Carpenter Square Alley and the name Willow Yang slipped from his memory like dead leaves.

1

On the evening of May 8, 1988, I left my riverside lodging as usual.

I closed the door carefully, doing my utmost to make no sound. I always made a point of differentiating myself from my ill-mannered neighbors, who shut their doors with a bang, as though they're chopping firewood. Then I stepped into the narrow street and its tawdry atmosphere.

The moon shone serenely overhead, but it was not high enough in the sky to cast its light directly onto the street. Instead the moonlight hung on the eaves of the houses on both sides, like early morning rain. So I walked along a street that looked as though it had been daubed with black paint, a street that triggered the same sense of disquiet as all the other streets, for darkness never gives me a full sense of security. The humdrum noises that fill the town during daylight hours become less intrusive in the quiet of evening, but still, like garish wildflowers, they aimed at me their vicious blooms.

In the street I met no one, making this the happiest excursion I had experienced until then. So I did not immediately turn into the broadest avenue in town that lay horizontally in front of me, but gazed back at my little street, still shrouded in darkness. The uneasiness I felt when first stepping outside had now subsided. The reason I lingered at the junction and did not proceed was that I couldn't be sure when I would next be walking along that street.

But I did not hesitate long. Someone—or, to be more

exact, someone's hazy shadow—appeared on the street, and the sounds of his footsteps were unusually loud. He was wearing the kind of shoes you can buy at any store, with metal toe taps nailed into them by some cobbler or other. I found the noise unbearable—someone might as well have been banging on my windows with a lump of scrap iron.

And thus my hesitation came to an abrupt end. I turned to my right, onto the broad avenue, and tried to quicken my pace, hoping that awful clatter would die a sudden death. But in front of me other dangers loomed: just as I was doing my best to shake off the footsteps behind, I had to dodge pedestrians in front of me, not to mention plane trees and trash cans and bicycles that appeared out of nowhere. Almost every evening outing involved me in this kind of arduous passage. Although the darkness gives me some cover, its protection is whittled away by the moonlight and the streetlamps. When a part of my body is exposed by the streetlamp, I feel a sudden pang of alarm. If I walk this street in daytime, when light is evenly distributed, I don't feel so conspicuous—though exposed, I am also hidden. But at night it's a different story. By this time I had passed the restaurant that had been redecorated multiple times and the shoe sounds behind had vanished, though I continued to be hemmed in by all kinds of noise. Given past experience, however, I knew that soon I would enter silence.

Before long I came to the street corner that would lead to the quiet part of town, and the issue facing me was how to cross the avenue in front of me so as to enter the little street opposite. Sometimes this crossing was an easy proposition, but at other times I would meet unexpected obstacles. Such was the case now, for two bicycles collided at the entrance to the very street I planned to enter. The two cyclists flew off their bicycles at different angles, but they were thrown to the ground in much the same way. Once they pulled themselves to their feet, each of them issued angry shouts of accusation, as loud as car engines starting up. Their clamor attracted people on all sides, and soon the intersection was so clogged you might have thought a sinkhole had just opened up. I was repelled by the crowd's excitement; its raucous din sounded like a hand grenade exploding. But soon the mob began to move to one side, like a huge toad lumbering its way forward, and finally the intersection opened up and I was able to cross the street.

Now I was on the street that led to my neighborhood—a concrete road sloping downhill toward a narrow crossroads that looked idle and unoccupied under the light of the streetlamps, announcing the silence beyond.

In the moonlight the buildings looked awkward and silly, the lights in their windows hinting at countless lives and giving me a comforting sense that they were holding in captivity all the people I didn't like. But their incarceration was not entirely assured: as I passed I could sometimes hear faint noises from the stairs inside, and I found this casual freedom of movement far from satisfactory. Entering the neighborhood, I could not avoid running into other pedestrians, or even bicycles and cars. But it was the pedestrians who worried me most, for whenever I thought of how their shoes were stepping on places where my feet had trod, I could not but feel a stab of pain.

I was now—as in the past—roaming free in the light projected through the curtains of my neighborhood. My fantasies darted around like bats, leading me into the unknown. I felt that I was leaving the neighborhood far behind and entering a place formed by innumerable strange rays of light.

But the situation at this moment on May 8, 1988, did not turn out as I would have liked. When my eyes lingered on a pair of curtains covered with arcs and circles, I didn't realize I was spending a bit too much time looking at them—I simply sensed that my train of thought was leaving the track it normally followed and heading off in another direction, as a path might do. A frightful notion was springing up in my mind, as I became aware that I was seeking to bypass the curtains, that I was bent on betraying them. The idea that had come into my head was this: The curtains represented a room, and the room ought to be occupied by at least one or two people, so what were they doing at this moment? This banal speculation gave me such a start, I knew I had to exit the neighborhood as soon as possible, and I quickened my pace accordingly. I dared not look up again at any curtains, as I was fearful that the blunder I had just committed might snowball into a disaster. I was hardly conscious of crossing the intersection, aware only that my emotions were beginning to stabilize. I proceeded up the slight incline and before long was back on the broad avenue.

The street was now much quieter. The shops had all shut for the night and just a few scattered people could be seen. Only now did I feel I was out of danger. The street was bathed in moonlight, and I felt I was treading the surface of a river that was placid, almost still.

I had just gotten as far as the restaurant when I heard something sounding in my inner heart. It came toward me steadily from the far distance and at first seemed much like tree leaves rustling in the wind, but later I gradually felt it was a lot like footsteps, as though someone were approaching me in my inner heart. This took me by surprise. In the time it took me to walk another ten meters, I could already make out that the footsteps were those of a young woman. She seemed to be walking barefoot in my heart, with steps as soft as bolls of cotton. I seemed to see faintly a little pair of pink feet, and my heart felt as warm as if it were bathed in sunshine. I kept on walking, and she seemed to be heading for the same place as I was. As I came to the end of the avenue and entered the narrow street, it felt as though we were strolling side by side.

It was in a blur of confusion that I reached my lodging. When I took out my key, I heard the sound of her taking out a key too. And then we inserted the keys into the locks at the same time, and simultaneously we released the latches and opened the doors. I went in, and so did she. What was different was that everything she did took place in my heart. When I closed the door, I heard the sound of her closing the door, and the sound of her closing the door was as gentle as the sound of her taking off her jacket. I stood in the room for a moment, and I felt her standing there too. The sound of her breathing was so minute, it called to mind the furrows formed by the wrinkles on my face. Then I went over to the window and opened it, and the breeze from the river blew into my room. I watched the river flowing and glimmering in the moonlight. I felt her standing by the window too, and together we watched the river in silence. Then I closed the window and went toward the bed. I sat on the bed for five minutes, then took off my coat and turned the light off. As I lay there, I watched how the moon shone in through the window and filled my bedroom with glistening light. She was lying in bed too, just as quietly as I was, but I could not determine exactly whether she was lying in my bed or another one. I felt that just like the moonlight I was immersed in the limitless quiet of night. Never before had I felt that everything was imbued with such an ineffable, wonderful atmosphere as it was now.

2

My uncanny experience on the evening of May 8 did not end with the passing of that night. As soon as I woke the following morning, I was conscious of an unfamiliarity in my surroundings, as though something had been added, or something taken away. This made me realize I was no longer on my own: another person had brought part of her life into mine. I felt no alarm on this account, nor was I carried away with joy. I accepted her coming just as I accepted the river that flowed past my lodging.

Lying in bed, I could sense that she had already left my inner world. She had risen when I was still asleep and was now making breakfast for me in the kitchen. I ignored the reality that there was no such room, for I could not persuade myself that no kitchen existed, given that she was in it. Her arrival had wrought a change in my living quarters.

I knew I ought to get up: it wouldn't do for me to still be lounging in bed when she already had breakfast made. Once up, the first thing I did was to open the curtains. I was still sleeping when she rose, so of course she had left them closed—that's the least a wife will do for a man. As I reached for the curtains, I realized there was no fabric for my hands to grip, and only then did I find that sunshine was already surging in. Outside, the river gleamed with unusual brightness and there were barges shimmering with light as they made their way along the channel. A few cabbage leaves floated past my window.

I walked toward the kitchen—knowing full well I did not have one—and went in. It was narrow, and I couldn't help rubbing against her on my way to the sink. I thought I heard her clothes rustle as I began to brush my teeth. She seemed to be saying something, but I wasn't sure what. I stopped my brushing and threw her a glance as soon as I realized my noise was drowning her out; she was looking at me, too. Her glance startled me, for up to this point she had existed only in my dim consciousness, but now I saw her glance in a very real way. Though I still could not get a full view of her eyes, her glance entered mine with unparalleled clarity. Her expression was calm—it had not annoyed her that I hadn't heard what she said—but her glance was aimed at me, signifying that she was awaiting my answer, or my question. I turned away in surprise, and for a moment I didn't know quite what to do. So her glance also shifted. Evidently, what she had said was of no special importance. As her glance moved away, I seemed to sense that her face was in motion. Then she left the kitchen.

Soon I left the kitchen too, and as I entered the bedroom I felt she was standing by the window. I went over and stood next to her. I tried to look at her glance from this angle, but could not see it clearly. She was gazing at the river below.

3

One afternoon many days later, I left my quarters. I had decided to go out for a while, because my living situation had begun to unsettle my nerves.

The girl who had come to me that evening and the glance she gave me the following day had caused my hitherto perfect life to acquire a blemish. Her glance roamed around my room the whole day through, but seldom could I actually see it. It was as though this girl who had only just come into my life had been my companion for a good twenty years, for she rarely looked at me and seemed much more inclined to gaze out the window. Her glance was always floating out of range, and I could never catch it. And so my exasperation grew with each new day.

On this particular afternoon I decided to subject her to a temporary abandonment. She stood by the window, gazing at the river that I had now come to resent. I moved toward the door, and as I did the whole room resounded with the weight of my shoes. Never before had I resorted to such loud footsteps, but I did so in order to make clear that I was leaving. I hoped that she would pay attention to me with her eyes, but when I reached the doorway and threw her a backward glance, she was still contemplating the river. This simply hardened my resolve. I opened the door and went out, closing the door with an even louder slam than my uncouth neighbors were wont to employ. I did not leave immediately, however, but opened the door once more. It seemed she was still standing by the window, impervious to my departure. When I closed the door a second time, the noise was just as dreary as my own mood, and as I walked away my steps sounded like dead tree limbs falling on the ground.

Once I was roaming the streets in broad daylight, I lost my customary wariness. On this first excursion in many days, I was not as circumspect as usual and no longer felt threatened by other pedestrians. Only now did it become fully apparent how lamentably her arrival had damaged my previous life. My footsteps felt disjointed and my glance was no longer on tentative lookout but had become as wild and uninhibited as a lunatic's, and I found myself taking a confrontational stance toward the tangle of glances aimed in my direction. Although I was hoping to fend off the glances of others, I could not contain my own desire to gaze, and as I walked on I did not avoid a single glance that came my way. For me to so hungrily meet these glances took me completely by surprise. Many eyes shrank away from mine, while a few seethed with hostility, but this did not make me hesitate in the slightest. When passing among these adversarial glances, I felt that my own gaze must surely appear very much at ease.

It gave me great satisfaction to stride down the street so assertively. When turning a corner or crossing the street, I no longer appeared hesitant but exhibited the same boldness that I would show if I were to toss pebbles into the river. I didn't know where exactly I was going, but I got the feeling that the glances on the street were growing fewer and I didn't come to a stop until I saw no glances at all, when I realized I was now in the residential part of town.

I was standing near an open door, and I saw a young man in a black jacket talking to an old woman who sat shelling beans in the doorway. Her voice made me think of an old newspaper flapping in the wind. Her gaze strayed outside my line of vision, and she did not look directly at the young man, either. Instead her eyes roamed between the beans and a utility pole; she seemed to be recounting to the young man some past episode whose details had grown fuzzy in her mind.

As I was about to leave, someone behind me uttered a brief sequence of sounds that clearly signified a person's name. When I turned my head, I saw that the speaker was another woman of much the same age as the first. The two women began to chatter in voices that seemed to have been pickled in salt, and their laughter sounded like two slabs of dried fish knocking against each other.

At this point the young man stood up—perhaps the woman's story was finished. He was much the same height as me. As he came my way he threw me a glance. To my astonishment, I found it was the same glance as the one I saw that time I had been brushing my teeth in the kitchen. He strode past me.

My surprise soon wore off, and as he walked on I realized what I needed to do next. I had no choice but to follow him.

The quiet with which he crossed the intersection gave me a warm, familiar feeling. Then he proceeded up the sloping concrete road, and I saw that his stride looked just like mine. Soon he reached the entrance to the main avenue, and he hesitated there for quite some time. I knew that he planned to cross the street, step onto the sidewalk opposite, and then head either left or right, but he needed to wait for a gap in the traffic. Suddenly he dashed across, and I rushed across at practically the same moment, because the opening had also presented itself to me. The panic he showed as he dashed across the street made me cringe with shame: for the first time I saw what an embarrassing figure I must have cut when I crossed the street before.

After this he recovered an appropriate degree of composure as he—and I—stepped onto the sidewalk, his newfound calm in turn making me feel very satisfied with my own gait. He proceeded forward in a most ordinary posture—precisely my own practice. Like me, he walked that way so as to make himself invisible. Now nobody noticed him, except for me. Watching him, I felt I was watching myself.

His walk terminated in front of a small, one-story house overlooking the river. From his right pocket he produced a yellow key—in my right pocket I too have a yellow key. He opened the door and went in. He appeared to close the door carefully, making as little noise as I usually made when I went out. But I did not enter this house by the river—I stood next to a concrete utility pole outside, in a welter of indecision. Because my following him had been purely involuntary, now that the pursuit had ended I was like a leaf that leaves its branch: once it touches ground it does not know what to do next. I felt that if I remained standing there I was liable to attract attention, so I strolled around a bit, at the same time trying to decide on my next step.

He emerged holding a sheaf of papers and a pencil. He closed the door and walked to his left; after a few more steps he turned the corner. Sidestepping a trash can, he went down the stairs toward the river. Then he clambered inside the arch of the concrete bridge. As he sat down, he appeared very much at ease.

I didn't follow him down the steps, because my indecision had not yet concluded. I was wondering why I was following him, and this question lingered in my mind for a long time before I came up with the answer: I had come here because of his glance. The trail had now reached its end, and he was sitting under the arch of the bridge. What should I do next? This question made me fretful. I walked back and forth on top of the bridge while the glance I saw days earlier in the kitchen was under the arch below. I began to imagine the things that might be attracting its attention: perhaps at this moment it was focused on a dirty, broken tile or lingering over a shred of moldy straw. When some barges emitting silly diesel-engine noises came chugging along the river, that glance was very likely fixed on their clouds of black smoke.

I decided to go inside the arch. The space should be able to accommodate two people, I thought. So I went down the slope of the bridge and followed the stone steps toward the river. I stood for a moment on the bank. He was sitting upright some ten meters away, his glance fixed on the paper he was holding. It was a more attractive scene than the one I had just been imagining. I walked toward him.

When he raised his head and looked at me, his glance made me a little nervous. But he did not show the slightest surprise; instead he eyed me calmly, making me feel that I was not approaching him rashly but responding to his invitation. I clambered inside the arch and sat down opposite him. I gazed into his eyes and confirmed that it was the same glance I saw in the kitchen. But his eyes were very different, I felt, from those of the girl. They were somewhat narrow, and it seemed to me that the girl's eyes were much wider.

"Some nights ago," I told him, "a young woman came into my heart. In some vague way she spent a whole evening with me. When I woke up the following morning, she was still there, and she let me see her glance. Her glance was just the same as your glance now."

4

After hearing my story, he raised none of the doubts that I had feared he might express. On the contrary, he seemed fully convinced that what I said was true.

"What you just told me," he said, "is very like something that happened to me ten years ago."

By "ten years ago," he explained, he meant May 8, 1988. On that night the moon shone enchantingly, and as usual he went out to wander the streets of his hometown. The street-lights were amber, and in their halo the moonlight seemed to drift down through the sky like drizzle. He walked along a street as tranquil as his own disposition, for it had long been his wont to go out late at night for a solitary stroll. He liked the expansive calm that he could find outside then. But that night something unexpected happened on this customary walk. For no reason at all he thought of a girl. He had been crossing a humpback bridge and had just stopped to watch the river as it flowed quietly along. It was when he was descending the bridge that the girl appeared in his mind, and so as he went down the incline his mind was full of wonder. He carefully inspected the image that he had seen, to discover that the girl was completely unfamiliar. Compared to the few women who had left an impression on him, she was clearly a different being altogether. He felt that for him to think for no reason of an utterly unknown young woman was somewhat baffling, and so he understood her appearance as a fleeting fantasy and felt that before long he would forget her, in the same way he would forget a piece of paper on which he had scrawled a few words. He began to head back toward his home, and the girl walked with him in his imagination. This time he was unsurprised, taking it for granted that before long she would voluntarily detach herself from his idle fancy. And so when he opened the door and she came in with him, he took it in stride. He went into his bedroom, threw off his coat, and lay down on the bed. He felt her lie down next to him, and a little smile appeared in the corner of his mouth. He was intrigued that the inspiration that had come to him on the bridge could be sustained until now. But he knew that when he woke up the next day she would be gone, and he fell asleep with complete peace of mind.

When he woke early the next morning, he immediately was aware of her—and even more clearly than the night before. He felt she had already risen, and it seemed she was in the kitchen. Lying in bed, he reviewed his experience of the previous night and discovered to his surprise that he could still confirm her existence in his imagination. And in his memory this experience was genuine, as though it had really happened.

"When I went into the kitchen that morning to brush my teeth, I saw her glance," he told me.

That was just the beginning. In the days that followed, he not only could not forget her but, on the contrary, in his imagination she became all the more clear and complete. Her eyes, nose, eyebrows, mouth, ears, and hair gradually emerged just as her glance had done, and all with unparalleled clarity, making him feel that she was truly standing right in front of him. But when he stretched out a hand to touch her, she was not there at all. He tried to sketch her image with a pencil on a piece of paper. Although he had never in his life learned to draw, within a month he could precisely and unerringly draw her face.

"She was such a pretty girl," he said.

He stuck the pencil drawing on the wall by the bed, and after that spent almost all his time gazing at it. Only when his father discovered that he had an eye disorder was he forced to abandon the portrait.

He was treated successively in three different hospitals, the last of which was in Shanghai. There, on the afternoon of August 14, he was wheeled into an operating room and surgery was performed. On September 1 the dressing was removed. That was when he learned that on the morning of August 14 a seventeen-year-old girl had been brought to the hospital after a car accident and had died in surgery at 3:16 that afternoon. Her eyes were extracted and the surgeon performed a corneal transplant. After his discharge on September 3 he did not go home, but traveled to the town of Smoke, having learned that was where the donor had lived.

His gaze fell on a willow tree on the riverbank and after a few moments of deep thought he gave a smile. "I remember now," he said. "The girl's name was Willow Yang."

But later he did not seek out the address he had been given and go knock on the black door of 26 Carpenter Square Alley. The change of plans came about because on the bus he had met a man named Shen Liang. Sketching the career of a Nationalist officer named Tan Liang, Shen told him how, during the evacuation in early 1949, ten time bombs were planted in Smoke.

On April 1, 1949, the day after Smoke was liberated, five of the bombs exploded, one after another. A People's Liberation Army platoon leader and a cook named Cui died in the explosions; thirteen PLA soldiers and twenty-one civilians (including five women and three children) were injured, some seriously.

The sixth bomb exploded in the spring of 1950, just as a public sentencing meeting was taking place in the playing field of the town's only school. Three mobsters had been earmarked for execution, and the bomb exploded underneath the stage that had been erected for the occasion. The condemned prisoners, along with the town mayor and three militiamen, flew into the sky in bits and pieces, and an old man named Li Jin still remembers how heads and arms and legs soared chaotically through clouds of smoke as a huge blast rent the air.

The seventh bomb detonated in 1960 in People's Park but inflicted no casualties, because the explosion occurred well after ten o'clock at night. As a testimony to the crimes of Chiang Kai-shek and the Nationalist Party, the park was left abandoned for the next eighteen years and was not restored until 1978.

The eighth bomb did not explode until the day that the young man in the black jacket and Shen Liang arrived in Smoke. Later the young man stood on the concrete bridge. Under a lowering sky the laborers dredging the river filled the riverbed like ants, forming a river of their own, though their flow was untidy and confused. As he listened to the hubbub that drifted up from the work site, he felt a heat flooding in from all sides and faintly heard the clang of metal on metal. A worker gave a cry of alarm and dashed toward the bank, struggling desperately because of the muddy ground, and soon all the laborers were fleeing pell-mell. That was how he came to witness the detonation of the eighth bomb.

A few days later he ran into Shen Liang a second time on the bridge. Shen Liang walked toward him in the bright sunshine, but the expression on his face made the young man think of an old wall covered in dust. Shen Liang came up to him and said, "I'm leaving."

He looked at Shen Liang silently. In fact, even as Shen Liang was approaching, he'd had a hunch that he was about to leave.

The two of them stood leaning against the balustrade for a long time. As day turned to night, Shen Liang told him about the eight bombs.

"There are still two that have not exploded," Shen Liang said.

In early 1949 Tan Liang had buried the ten bombs in an intricate geometric pattern. Shen Liang explained this to him one more time, adding: "All it takes is for one more bomb to go off, and the location of the tenth bomb can be worked out from the positions of the previous nine."

But two bombs had yet to explode, and so Shen Liang said, "Even Tan Liang himself would be unable to determine their location at this point.

"Thirty-nine years have passed, after all," he said.

After that, Shen Liang just stood gazing silently at the town of Smoke. It was only as he left that he spoke once more: he said the moonlight was trickling down like water.

In the late afternoon of September 15, 1971, the boiler of the fertilizer plant suddenly exploded with a deafening roar. Five bystanders who witnessed the explosion from a distance said that after the boiler blasted into the sky it shattered into countless pieces like a broken bottle.

Wu Dahai, the boilerman on duty that evening, was lucky not to have been blown up. He was squatting in the toilet when the explosion occurred, and the huge blast knocked him unconscious. He died in 1980 of congestive heart failure, and on the eve of his death the sight of the boiler blowing up replayed itself in his mind. He told his wife that before the boiler flew into the air and exploded, he distinctly heard a detonation underground.

"In fact, that was a bomb going off," said the young man in the black jacket. "The boiler obscured the true facts. So now it's just the last bomb that has yet to explode."

Then he said, "Just now I was talking about the boiler incident with an old woman who lives nearby. She's Wu Dahai's widow."

1

The girl who arrived on the evening of May 8 and revealed her glance the following morning soon made herself part of my existence. Two people now figured in my far-from-spacious life.

In the days that followed I would spend practically all my time in my chair, feeling her move around the room. On good days, in a relaxed mood, she would sit on the bed and gaze at me with that glance I found so captivating. But more often she seemed restless. She so loved to potter about the room, it felt like there was a night breeze constantly blowing back and forth. I tolerated this disregard of my existence and did my best to find excuses for her behavior. I did concede that my room was a bit on the small side and I understood her constant movement as a sign that the room might become a bit bigger. But my self-restraint did not move her in the slightest; she seemed utterly indifferent to the fact that I was expending considerable energy just to keep a lid on my annoyance. In the end her insensitivity stirred me to rage, and one day as dusk approached I bellowed at her, "That's enough of that! If you want exercise, go outside."

These words must have hurt her, for she went over to the window at once. Gazing at the river, she conveyed her unhappiness and disappointment. But I too was discouraged. If at that moment she had bolted out the door, I think I would not have stood in her way. That evening I went to bed early but fell asleep late. I lay there brooding, recalling the wonderful life I used to have and lamenting that it had been ruined by her arrival. For hours my anger blazed. As I drifted off to sleep, she was still standing by the window. I felt that when I woke up the following day there was a good chance she would be gone: ultimately she should be capable of executing a permanent departure, and I would neither miss her nor feel the slightest regret. I seemed to see a green leaf falling from a tree, yellowing on the ground, and finally decomposing into the soil. For me, her arrival and departure would be just like that leaf's passage.

But when I woke in the morning, I could sense that she had not left after all. She was sitting by the bed, her eyes resting on me from time to time, and I sensed that she had sat there the whole night. She gazed at me so enchantingly, it made me feel as though there had never been any friction between us, and my anger of the previous night now seemed an utter sham. Never before had she looked at me in such a sustained way, and so as I returned her gaze I could not help but feel nervous, afraid that she might direct it elsewhere. I lay on the bed not daring to move, lest she sense that something had happened in the room and turn her gaze away. Now I needed to maintain absolute stillness—for only thus would she not divert her gaze, only thus might she possibly forget that she was looking at me.

Her sustained attention made me feel that I was gradually seeing her eyes. I seemed to see her gaze grow and spread, and thus her eyes were slowly revealed. At that point a dark mist appeared in front of my own eyes, but I saw her eyes clearly nonetheless, and as they appeared, so too did her eyebrows. Only now did I understand how her glance could be so beguiling: it was because her eyes were so graceful and attractive. Then her nose became visible: I seemed to see a water droplet fall from the tip of her nose. And then I saw her lips, moist lips that thrilled me to the core. A few strands of hair hung down by the corners of her mouth, like willow fronds on a riverbank, and then all her hair came into view. Her face was now detailed and complete. The only thing I couldn't see were her ears, for they were concealed by her tresses. Black hair fell quietly around her face, and I was tempted to stretch out a hand to touch it but didn't dare, fearing that all might suddenly disappear. It was then I discovered that tears were wetting my cheeks.

From that day on, I was constantly shedding tears. My eyes

ached the whole day through, and I kept feeling there must be a bunch of unripe grapes in some corner of the room. I began to sense that changes had taken place in my home. My bed and chair gradually lost their firmness and seemed to swell like rising dough. A fortnight had passed since I last saw the lovely spectacle of moonlight shining in, and during the day I found the sunlight dark. Sometimes I would stand by the window and hear the sound of the river below, but I could not make out where its banks were and I was left with a feeling that the river had widened enormously. As my tears fell, she no longer paced the room as she had before. She began to linger quietly by my side, seemingly aware of my pain and racked with worry.

As the objects around me grew blurred, she became more distinct. When she sat in the chair, I seemed to see her left foot slightly raised, the top of her white sock peeping out above her black leather shoe. She wore a long dress, in colors I found dazzling—I was unable to distinguish them in detail. It made me recall the bright curtains hanging in the windows of my neighbors, and those pictures in my mind in turn led me back to her dress. Later, I was even able to gauge her height: she looked to be 1.65 meters tall. I don't know how I came up with that figure, but I felt sure it was correct.

After a fortnight, my eyes no longer watered. I woke up one morning to find the pain had gone and everything had grown quiet. She was in the kitchen, it seemed, as I lay in bed watching the murky sunlight seep in from outside. From the river came the pure sound of a boat's scull cleaving the water, bringing a melodious note to the peace I felt and giving me a refreshing confidence that my health was on the mend: turbulence had flowed away into the distance, leaving a permanent calm. I knew that my past life had gone on too long and that now had come the moment to make a new start. Thanks to her, fresh blood was flowing in my veins; out of what once had been a clump of weeds, a gorgeous flower had emerged. From this time on, my lodging would be imbued with twin energies, harmoniously connected.

I felt her come out of the kitchen and move toward me, radiating happiness, for it seemed that she knew the pain in my eyes had gone and had heard every word of my inner monologue. She came over and sat down on my bed, an indication that she agreed completely with my thoughts. Her look told me she wanted to join me in designing our future, and this desire was entirely appropriate, this emotional investment was exactly what I was hoping to see. And so we began to discuss things.

I asked her several times what she was thinking. She never replied, but simply looked at me without saying a word. Later I realized that her idea was the same as my idea. So I began to look around the room. The first thing I noticed was the absence of curtains. Window coverings were needed, I felt. Life was not the same anymore: in the past I had been brazen and unabashed, but now she and I would have our secret affairs, and such affairs called for the screening that curtains provide.

"We should have curtains," I said.

She nodded, I felt.

"Do you like the color of grass?" I asked. "Or do you prefer the color of flowers?"

I could sense that she liked the color of grass. I found her answer pleasing, for I liked that color too. So I sat up and told her I would go out right away and buy curtains the color of grass. She stood up too, seemingly appreciative of my resolve, and I felt her move contentedly toward the kitchen. I jumped out of bed, and when I'd put some clothes on and was going out the door, I seemed to pass the kitchen and see her with her back to me, though what I saw was more like a shadow, dim and unclear, on the wall. I slipped quietly out the door, hoping to come back shortly with the curtains—ideally, even before she realized I was gone.

And so, as I stepped into the little street outside my residence, I had no reason to repeat the tentative kind of walk that had formerly been my custom. Recalling how a bicycle can zip off in no time at all, I aimed to be just as nimble and speedy. Although I kept bumping into people as I strode along the hazy streets, this did not make me slow down, and when I reached the crossroads I felt that the mist was beginning to lift. It occurred to me that once we had curtains hanging in my residence, when we opened them in the morning it would perhaps be just as light as it was now.

Although a brightness had appeared in front of me, things remained indistinct, but I knew I was now walking on the broad avenue. I heard a clamor on all sides, surging toward me like a tide. I could faintly make out streets, houses, trees, pedestrians, and vehicles, but all had taken on an unfamiliar aspect: flabby, they glimmered with an ambiguous light. And the shapes of the pedestrians had grown strange and anomalous: although each individual walked separately, the vague glow lumped them all together. As I threaded my way among them, I could not help being cautious. Confused by the uncertain light, I was afraid I would stumble into a huge cobweb and never be able to extricate myself. But my zigzag advance went rather smoothly: apart from several unavoidable collisions, my progress was never interrupted.

Before long I arrived at the place that in the past had always made me hesitate. I needed to cross the main street and get to the other side; from there I would follow a narrow side street to what was always a quiet intersection.

This crossing was not, in fact, a complicated proposition. But on reaching the middle of the street, I suddenly realized that to cross it made no sense at all—carrying on in that direction would take me back to the residential area, when I had come out specifically to buy curtains. I didn't reproach myself—I simply turned around and headed back. No sooner did I take a second step than I was thrown into the air by the impact of a hard, solid vehicle, and the next thing I knew, I'd hit the ground. I heard the crisp snap of bones breaking and felt the blood in my veins thrown into chaos, as though a riot had erupted.

2

The sun was shining on the afternoon of September 2, 1988, as I sat next to a raised flower bed in the courtyard of a Shanghai hospital. Holding a clump of grass between my fingers, I watched as a nurse with no wrinkles on her face walked slowly toward me.

I had been replaying in my mind all that had happened since I went off into town to buy curtains. My morning had ended with a traffic accident: I was knocked senseless by a Liberation truck and packed off to the hospital in Smoke.

As I was recovering from my injuries, an ophthalmologist came into my ward looking for a surgeon and noticed that my vision was severely impaired. She sat down by my sickbed and warned me that without treatment I was in danger of losing my sight altogether. Once I was able to get up, they crammed me into a white ambulance and I was delivered to the hospital in Shanghai. On August 14, three eye doctors performed a corneal transplant. On September 1, the gauze on my eyes was removed, and I felt that everything around me had recovered its former clarity.

Now the nurse was standing by my side and looking at me with young and buoyant eyes as the sunshine danced on her white scrubs. I caught a whiff of surgical dressings and ethyl alcohol.

"Why are you holding a clump of grass?" she asked.

I did not answer, because I did not understand the question.

"There are so many lovely flowers," she said. "Why do you prefer grass?"

"I really don't know," I said.

She laughed. Her laughter made me think of a kindergarten in Smoke that I had once walked past.

"There was a girl named Willow Yang—she's not with us anymore," she said. "The last time I saw her, she was sitting where you are now, a clump of grass in her hand. I asked her the same question that I just asked you, and she gave me exactly the same answer."

I must not have displayed sufficient interest in her remarks, for she went on, "The look in her eyes was just like that in yours."

Our conversation continued for some time. The nurse told me the story of how seventeen-year-old Willow Yang had been admitted to the hospital with leukemia and died shortly after my arrival. It was she who gifted me the corneas that restored my sight. She died a little after three o'clock on August 14, just as the hospital was awaiting a donor.

The nurse pointed at a five-story building in front of us. "Before she died, Willow Yang was up on the fourth floor, next to the window."

My bed was precisely two floors below. I realized that I had been lying in the same location as she, except with one floor in between.

"Who is in the bed by the third-floor window?" I asked.

"I'm not sure," she said.

When she left, I went on sitting by the flower bed, the clump of grass still in my hand. I began to think about the girl named Willow Yang; I was trying to imagine the expression on her face as death approached. This train of thought held me in its grip for a long time, and so when I was settling my bill with the hospital cashier I took the opportunity to inquire about the girl's place of residence. She lived in Smoke, at 26 Carpenter Square Alley. I wrote her address on a piece of paper and slipped it into the left pocket of my jacket.

3

After my release from the hospital on September 3, I boarded a long-haul bus bound for Smoke.

It was an overcast morning, and as the bus drove along Shanghai's dark streets, heavy banks of cloud covered the tops of the few high-rise buildings. The scene outside the window conjured a picture in my mind of a monotonous expanse of gray-tiled roofs. I reminded myself that I would soon be in Smoke, and visualized how at midday I would take out a key and insert it into the lock on my door. And so as I sat in the bus I could not avoid the sight of her sitting in the chair in the room. My mind was as still as a dry riverbed, and my passion was spent. I knew that when I entered my lodging she would rise from the chair, but I did not imagine the form in which she would express her feelings. I would nod in her direction, and nothing else would happen. It would be as though I had not been away long, but had simply gone out for a stroll. And she would not have just recently arrived—it would be as though she had lived with me for twenty years. Tired from the journey, I might well lie down in bed and fall asleep right away. Perhaps she would stand by the window as I fell asleep. Everything would happen in utter silence, and I hoped this silence could be sustained indefinitely.

Once the bus got clear of Shanghai, I saw broad fields, and the black clouds extended endlessly, roaming at will across the landscape. The drab colors outside the window did little to raise my spirits.

Inside the bus voices swayed back and forth, knocking against one another like discarded bottles. I was sitting by the aisle, in seat 27. In seat 25, next to the window, sat an old man wearing a dark blue jacket. A somewhat fishy odor wafted from his direction. In the middle, in seat 26, sat a young man who seemed to have traveled far and whose manner evoked an expanse of green grass dancing in the breeze. We were besieged by a hubbub of voices. The outlander looked out the window, while the old man was lost in thought, his eyes closed.

The bus sped along under the lowering sky. Before long it stopped in Jinshan, and then it set off again. The old man by the window now opened his eyes and turned his head to look at the passenger in seat 26, who continued to face the window—I couldn't tell whether he was looking at the scenery outside or at the old man next to him.

At this point I heard the old man say, "My name is Shen Liang."

His voice continued. "I'm from Zhoushan."

He added, with particular emphasis, "It's the first time in my life I ever left Zhoushan."

After that he said nothing more, but he maintained the posture in which he had been while talking. It was not until some forty minutes later, as the bus was approaching Smoke, that he spoke again. His voice now sounded different.

He told the outlander an old, old story—how, in early 1949, a Kuomintang military officer named Tan Liang had directed sappers to plant ten time bombs in Smoke.

The story unspooled like a highway that extends to the far horizon, and the old man's voice was slow and unhurried. It was only when Smoke could dimly be seen in the distance that he brought his narrative to an abrupt halt and his eyes turned to the scene outside the window.

The bus drove into the station in Smoke. The three of us were the last travelers to leave the station. Outside, several people were waiting to meet passengers. Two men were smoking; a woman was greeting a man on a bicycle. We left the station together and must have gone some twenty meters when the old man came to a stop. He stood there, looking at the town with a strange expression on his face, while the outlander and I continued on our way. Later the outlander stopped to talk to a young woman standing by the side of the road, and I went on alone.

1

Much later, when I looked back once more at the events that began on the evening of May 8, 1988, the image of the young woman would vividly emerge before me. All those early scenes appeared very real in my later recollections. The result was that I believed more and more firmly that a young woman had truly appeared in my life, and not in my imagination. At the same time I realized clearly that these things had all happened in the past, and now, as before, I had nothing. Once again I resumed my former life. Almost every night I walked around the neighborhood and bathed in the curtain light. What was different was that in the daytime, too, I would roam boldly through the streets where ordinary people milled about. Now I no longer felt a danger if others smiled at me— and nobody was smiling at me in any case.

In my sparse memory, the episodes relating to the young lady were limited in duration, beginning with her first appearance on May 8 and ending with the unfortunate traffic accident. All that happened afterward was transmuted into a series of dark nights with no moon. My mood now as I wandered the streets was much like that of a bereaved husband, and as time stole by I began to accept that the wife I once had had died a long time ago.

Later, one day I quite by accident came across a yellowed sheet of paper on which was written: Willow Yang, 26 Carpenter Square Alley.

I had been sitting at my desk and for some reason I can't explain I opened a drawer that I had not rummaged through in years, and in it found this piece of paper.

The characters written there pointed me toward some hazy episode in my past, and for a while I engaged in fruitless musing. Then my eyes fixed on the sunshine outside my window, and I connected that sunlight with all the other sunlight that still lingered in my memory. In so doing, I summoned back the sunshine that had warmed a courtyard next to a gaily-colored flower bed. A nurse walked toward me in the bright sun and her lips made enchanting shapes as she told me about a girl named Willow Yang.

The appearance of the yellowed paper at this moment served as a cue. Long ago, when I scribbled those words at the hospital, I didn't really know my own mind—recording the address was purely a reflex action. Only with the paper's resurfacing at this juncture did I understand what had led me to do so. Now, as I left the sunshine by my window and entered the sunshine in the street, I knew exactly where I was going.

The black door of 26 Carpenter Square Alley was mottled with age. When I knocked, I detected the tiny sound of flakes of paint falling to the ground, and this patter continued off and on for some time before hesitant footsteps could be heard inside. The door emitted a decrepit creak, and a man in his fifties stood before me. A look of surprise appeared on his face.

I felt embarrassed by my presumption.

But he said, "Come in." It was as though he had known me for ages and simply hadn't expected me to turn up at this moment.

"Are you the father of Willow Yang?" I asked.

He did not answer directly. "Come in," he repeated.

I followed him inside, and after crossing a moss-covered courtyard we entered a south-facing room. It was furnished with several traditional-style wooden chairs, and I chose the one that was closest to the window. It felt a bit damp when I sat down. He looked at me with the gaze of an old acquaintance, maintaining the same composure he had shown when opening the door. His calm demeanor would make it easier for me to explain my purpose in coming.

"Your daughter—" I began.

I tried hard to recall the shapes formed by the lips of the nurse by the flower bed. "Your daughter died on August fourteenth, 1988?"

"That's right," he said.

"On that day I was lying on an operating table in the same Shanghai hospital," I told him. I was hoping that his self-command would last another five minutes, for that way I could fit in all the elements of my story, from the traffic accident, through his daughter's donation of her eyes, to the successful transplant.

But he did not let me continue. "She did not go to Shanghai," he said. "In all her seventeen years she never once went to Shanghai."

I was unable to conceal my puzzlement. My eyes must have been full of doubt.

Still he looked at me calmly. "But it's true that she died on August fourteenth, 1988," he went on.

He would never forget that sweltering afternoon. He and Willow had eaten their lunch in the courtyard. "I feel tired," she told him.

He noticed her face was pale and suggested she have a nap.

His daughter stood up, looking out of sorts, and made her way shakily into her bedroom. She had seemed a bit distracted before, so he didn't worry unduly and simply felt a loving concern for her.

Once in her room, she said through the window, "Please wake me at three thirty."

He said he would do so, and then seemed to hear her murmur, "I feel I could fall asleep and never wake up."

He did not pay particular attention to this remark. It was only later, when he recalled these last words, that he realized they were a signal. Her voice at that moment already sounded faint and unreal.

That afternoon he did not have a nap but simply stayed in the courtyard reading the newspaper. When it came around to 3:30, he entered her bedroom to find she was no longer breathing.

He pointed toward the room facing me. "That's where Willow died."

I had to believe him. A father who has lost his daughter would not joke about this, I thought.

"Would you like to see her room?" he asked, after a long pause.

His question took me aback, but I responded in the affirmative.

So together we went into her room. It was dark, and I noticed that the curtains, the color of green grass, were tightly drawn. He turned on the light.

I noticed two framed pictures next to the bed. One was a color photograph of a young woman's face, and the other was a pencil drawing of a young man. I looked closely at the photograph, to find that the young woman in the picture was the very same one who had entered my heart so many years ago on May 8. As I gazed at her photo, an image of her turning her face toward me was superimposed on this picture. And so once more I felt that my past was very real.

"Do you see my daughter's gaze?" he asked me.

I nodded. I saw the eyes of my departed wife.

"Don't you feel that her gaze is very much like yours?"

It took me a moment to register what he said.

So he added, somewhat apologetically, "In the photo, maybe her gaze is a little blurry."

Then, as if to make up for that, he pointed at the pencil portrait. "A long time ago," he said, "when Willow was still living, all of a sudden one day she thought of a boy she did not know and had never seen. As time went on he kept appearing ever more distinctly in her imagination, and she ended up sketching his portrait."

His account of the pencil sketch's origins seemed to match my own past experience, so my glance left the girl in the color photo and rested instead on the pencil sketch. The person I saw there was not me but a totally unfamiliar young man.

As Willow's father saw me out the door, he said, "You know something? I noticed you a long time ago, when you were living in a cottage by the river. Your gaze was just like my daughter's."

2

Once I left 26 Carpenter Square Alley, the encounter I had just had—and the voice of that middle-aged man—now seemed things from the distant past. And so, as I left the girl in the color photo, my emotions were not particularly stirred. Everything that had just happened seemed like a repeat of a past event, a little like me sitting by the window in my room and recalling the scene on the evening of May 8. All that was new was the door with the peeling black paint, the man in his fifties, and the two framed pictures. My wife died on August 14, 1988: as I walked along, I rehearsed this stale old line.

When I entered the street that ran parallel to the river, I noticed a young man walking toward me. In the bright sunshine his black jacket assumed a strange gaiety, and somehow I found myself watching his every move. He entered a little house overlooking the river, but before long he came out again, holding a pencil and a sheaf of papers. He went down the steps toward the river and made his way under the arch of the bridge and sat down.

For a reason I cannot explain, I too descended the steps. He showed no sign of disapproval as he saw me approaching, so I joined him under the arch. He pushed aside some sheets of paper that were lying on the ground, and I sat down. I noticed that the papers were covered with a complicated grid of lines.

Our conversation began a minute later. He knew, perhaps, that I would listen quietly, however long he talked.

"Here in this town in early 1949," he began, "a Nationalist officer named Tan Liang had ten time bombs buried in an intricate geometric pattern."

His story stretched from 1949 until the present. During that period, nine bombs had gone off. "There is still one that has not exploded," he told me.

He picked up the sheets of paper. "That bomb is now buried in ten places."

The first place was in the cinema, beneath the third seat in the ninth row. "That seat is a bit dilapidated," he said, "and the springs are showing." The other nine locations were as follows: underneath the front door of the bank; the crossroads leading to the residential area; next to the crane at the cargo wharf; the hospital morgue (a dumb place to leave a bomb, in his view); by the second plane tree over from the entrance to the department store; the kitchen of room 102 in the machine factory dormitory; beneath the main road, sixteen meters from the bus station; immediately outside 57 Carpenter Square Alley; and directly below the fifth window to the right of the Workers' Club Dance Hall.

After he had finished his recital, I asked, "Are you saying that there are ten bombs in the town?"

"That's right." He nodded. "And they could go off at any time."

Now I realized why he had caught my attention and why I'd felt the urge to sit down with him. It was because he made me think of the pencil sketch in Willow Yang's bedroom: the subject of that portrait was now sitting opposite me.

Love Story

The autumn of 1977 left a mark on two young people. On a day when the sun was shining they boarded a clattering bus and traveled to a town twenty kilometers away. It was the boy who bought the tickets, while the girl took cover behind a concrete utility pole some distance from the station. Dust and falling leaves fluttered around her and the hum of the power lines dulled the multitude of noises in the street. The girl's emotions at that moment were as barren as a page in one of her school textbooks. She glanced from time to time at the bus station's narrow door, a placid expression on her face.

The boy emerged, looking wan and haggard. Although he knew perfectly well where the girl was hiding, he avoided looking her way and instead walked toward the river, scanning nervously left and right. Soon he reached the bridge and came to an uneasy halt before finally gazing in the girl's direction. Finding that she was watching him, he glared at her, but this seemed to have no effect. He turned away in disgust and then stood where he was, ignoring her. But he felt certain that she was looking at him the whole time, and this thought alarmed him. Only when he was sure there was nobody around did he walk back.

She had no inkling that he was in such a fearful state of mind; instead she felt touched by the sight of the pale boy walking toward her in the sunshine. A quiver of excitement seized her and a smile appeared on her face. But when he arrived beside her, he was fuming. "You can still smile?" he snapped.

Her lovely smile was nipped in the bud. So fierce was his expression that she looked at him anxiously, hoping for clarification.

"How many times do I have to tell you?" he said. "Don't look at me. Pretend you don't know me. Why do you keep looking? You drive me crazy."

She made no protest and simply turned away. She looked at a pile of withered yellow leaves on the ground and listened as sounds emerged from his mouth.

"After we get on the bus, find a seat and sit down. If there's nobody we know, I'll sit next to you. If there *is* someone we know, I'll stand by the door. Remember not to talk to me."

He handed her a ticket and walked away—back toward the bridge, not the waiting room.

Some ten years later, the girl—now in her late twenties—sat opposite me as twilight fell outside our apartment and the open curtains framed the sun's fading light. She was knitting a sky-blue scarf. The scarf was longer than she was tall, but still she kept on knitting. It was I who had accompanied her in the autumn of 1977 to that town twenty kilometers away. We were five years old when we first met, and that acquaintance eventually led—after a long and grueling process—to the institution of marriage. We had our first sexual experience near the end of our sixteenth year, and her first pregnancy occurred at that time too. Her sitting posture had repeated itself endlessly for five years, so how could there be any passion in my glance when I looked at her? For so long now, wherever I went she would follow, and this put me in a profound depression. My biggest mistake was that on the eve of our wedding I had failed to realize that all her life she would be hanging on my coattails, and that was why I was stuck in such a rut. Now, as she knitted the scarf, I held in my hand a letter from the author Hong Feng. His splendid career was an inspiration to me, and I felt I had no reason to continue a life as stale as an old newspaper.

So, just as she recycled her sitting position, I recycled words I had said before, reiterating that there was something awful about knowing someone since childhood. "Don't you feel I'm just too familiar?" I asked yet again.

But she just kept gazing at me uncomprehendingly.

"We have known each other since we were five," I went on. "Twenty-some years later, we're still together. How can either of us expect the other to be able to inspire a change?"

At such moments she would always look stricken.

"To me, for ages now you have been like a blank piece of paper that can be read at a glance. And to you, aren't I just the same?"

When tears began to spill down her face, I thought she simply looked foolish.

"All that we're left with," I went on, "is memories of the past, but too many memories make our past seem just like breakfast—always predictable."

Our first sexual experience, as I said, occurred near the end of our sixteenth year. On that moonless night, we lay locked in an embrace on the grass of the school athletic field, paralyzed with fear. On a path not far away, people walked along with flashlights in their hands, their voices sharp as daggers in the night air, and several times we were about to flee in panic. When I recall that scene today, I realize that it was because she hugged me so tightly that I now cannot see just how pathetic I must have looked then.

As soon as I think of that night, I can feel the moisture of the dewdrops on the grass. When I slipped my hand inside her pants, the heat of her body made me shiver. My fingers dipped deeper, and I began to feel a wetness just like that on the grass. At the beginning I had no particular purpose in mind and simply felt like caressing her a little bit. Later I felt a strong urge to take a peek—I wanted to know what things looked like. But on that moonless night, what I smelled when I leaned closer was only a bland scent. The scent that wafted from that dark, wet place wasn't like anything I had smelled before, but it wasn't nearly as exciting as I had imagined it would be. That did not stop me, however, from going ahead and doing the deed. Desire had been sated, only to leave me racked with anxiety, and in the days that followed I considered various forms of suicide or flight. When she began to look pregnant, my despair was paired with resentment that I had enjoyed only a few minutes of earthshaking bliss. On that autumn day in 1977 I accompanied her to that town twenty kilometers away in the hope it would all prove to be a false alarm.

Her fear was not nearly as acute as mine. When I proposed she have a checkup, it was she who suggested that particular hospital, and her calm and coolheadedness took me rather aback. To me, the attraction of that facility was simply that it represented a basic level of security that would allow us to keep the matter secret. But she went on to enthuse about her visit to that town five years earlier, and I was infuriated by her descriptions of its streets and her lyrical accounts of the decommissioned ship that was moored by the shore. We weren't going there to have fun, I told her, but for a damn checkup, a test that would determine whether or not we could go on living. If the test established that she really was pregnant, I said, we would be expelled from school and driven from our homes by our respective sets of parents. Rumors about us would proliferate like the dust that blew about in the streets. In the end there would be nothing for it but to . . . "Commit suicide."

That threat certainly did unnerve her. The look on my face, she told me years later, was quite terrifying, and my prediction of our grim future shocked her. But even in this apprehensive state she was never really in despair. At least *her* parents wouldn't expel her from the family home, she believed, although she did concede that they would punish her. "Punishment's better than suicide," she told me consolingly.

That day I was the last person to get on the bus. I watched her from a distance as she boarded, and she kept turning around and looking at me. I had told her not to do that, but my constant reminders had fallen on deaf ears. The bus was already lurching forward when I boarded. I didn't immediately head for the seat next to hers but stood by the door, my eyes scanning one face after another, and there must have been at least twenty people I had seen before. So I stood glued to my spot, as the potholed highway toyed relentlessly with our bus. I felt as though I were stuffed inside a bottle that was being constantly shaken. Later I heard her calling me—a sound that filled me with dread. Outraged by her lack of sense, I steadfastly ignored her, hoping that would shut her up. But her tiresome efforts to catch my attention just carried on regardless. All I could do was turn my head away, knowing my scowl had to be as ugly as the scrubby bushes by the side of the road.

But her face was suffused with innocence as she put on a show of being astonished that she and I just happened to have taken the same bus. When she invited me to sit down in the empty seat next to her, I had no choice but to comply. No sooner did I sit down than I could feel her body pressing up against me. She had a lot to say, but I didn't take any of it in and had to keep nodding in order to give the impression I was following what she was saying. All this exasperated me, and when she quietly curled her hand around my fingers, I pushed her hand away. It maddened me that she could still carry on like this. Only then did she register how furious I was. She stopped talking, and naturally gave up on efforts at physical contact too. She turned away, feeling mistreated it seemed, and began to survey the bleak scenery. But she did not stay quiet for very long, for when the bus shuddered as it went over a bump she gave a giggle and murmured in my ear, "The baby felt that."

Her joke only provoked me further. "Shut your mouth," I muttered, through clenched teeth.

Later I saw a row of ships moored by the shore. Two of them had been stripped down to miserable-looking shells, and only one was still intact and undamaged. A few gray birds hovered over the seaweed on the shore.

Soon after the bus arrived at the station, two young people emerged from the exit. When a truck drove past, their bodies were obscured by the dust it threw up.

The boy, livid, walked on ahead without a word. The girl followed along behind, glancing apprehensively at his side-turned face. Instead of heading straight for the hospital, the boy turned into an alleyway, and the girl did the same. He did not stop until halfway down. There they watched as a middle-aged woman approached and then walked out onto the street.

"Why did you call me?" the boy barked.

The girl, hurt, looked at him. "I was afraid you'd get tired standing all the way."

"How many times have I told you: don't look at me!" he cried. "But you just kept on looking and calling my name and squeezing my hand."

Two men approached from the end of the alley. The boy said nothing more, and the girl made no attempt to defend herself. The men looked at them curiously as they passed. Then the boy set off toward the end of the alley, and after a slight hesitation the girl followed.

They walked in silence along the street. Though no longer in a rage, the boy seemed increasingly fretful as they approached the hospital. He threw a glance at the girl, who was now gazing straight ahead, and he inferred from the look of hesitancy in her eyes that the hospital must be very close.

They arrived at the hospital lobby to find the registration office empty and desolate. The boy now lost his nerve so completely that he marched straight outside to the courtyard. Gripped by a fear that he might be held for questioning, he was simply not prepared to run the risk. She would have to confront the dangers alone, leaving him free to make his escape. By the time the girl joined him, he had thought of a way to conceal his spinelessness. It would really be too dangerous for him to stay with her, he said: other people would be able to tell in an instant what they had got up to. "Just go in by yourself," he told her.

She made no protest and with a nod headed back inside. He watched as she went up to the window of the registration office, and when she took money from her pocket she showed no obvious stress. He heard her provide name and age—both were fake. These subterfuges were not things he had arranged ahead of time. "Gynecology," he heard her say.

The word made him shudder. He detected a weariness in her voice. On leaving the window, she turned to look at him, and the medical record flapped in her hand as she went up the stairs.

The boy watched until her silhouette disappeared on the stairs; only then did he turn his gaze elsewhere. He felt his mood getting darker, and his breathing became labored. As he stood waiting, he looked out distractedly at the people on the street, then eyed the patients as they came down the stairs. Still no sign of her. He was seized with dread, a fear that upstairs his secret was being exposed. This thought became more and more real, until he couldn't bear to stay in the hospital a moment longer. He crossed the street and didn't stop when he got to the other side, but rushed straight into a shop.

It sold basic household supplies, and a slatternly young woman stood behind the counter, a bored expression on her face. At the other end were two men cutting sheets of glass. He went over to watch, at the same time glancing frequently at the hospital across the street. The men smoked as they worked, and little heaps of ash had accumulated on the dark green glass. The vacant looks on their faces made him all the more glum. As the cutting tool's diamond tip slid across the glass, a white scratch appeared and a rasping noise sounded in his ears.

Before long the girl appeared on the street opposite. She stood next to a plane tree, looking lost. He glimpsed her through the dusty shop window and did not step outside until he had verified that she was not being followed. She saw him crossing the street and gave a rueful smile as he approached. "I *am* pregnant," she said quietly.

The boy stood as still as a tree. The desperate hope he had been harboring was now utterly shattered. He looked at the doleful girl. "What are we going to do?"

"I don't know," she muttered.

"What do we do?" he repeated.

"Let's not think about that," she said consolingly. "Let's have a look around the shops."

He shook his head. "I don't feel like it."

She said nothing, and simply watched the traffic going back and forth on the street. People came toward them on the sidewalk, laughing loudly. After they passed, she gave it another try. "Let's have a look in the shops."

"I don't want to do that," he repeated.

They stood there for some time, and eventually the boy said listlessly, "Let's go back."

The girl nodded.

So then they headed back the way they had come. Before they had gone very far, the girl came to a stop in front of a window. She tugged on the boy's sleeve. "Let's have a look in this shop," she said.

After a little hesitation the boy entered with her. They stood for a while in front of a white Dacron skirt. The girl could not take her eyes off it. "I really like that skirt," she told the boy.

Her voice had already settled into place when she was sixteen. In the ten-odd years that followed, her voice would linger in my ears almost every day, and this overfamiliar sound had scoured away all my passion. And so, as dusk fell and I gazed at my wife who sat opposite me, I could only feel more and more weary. She was still knitting the sky-blue scarf, and her face was the same old face, except that it had lost some elasticity. Under my glances her wrinkles had deepened and were now as familiar to me as the palm of my own hand. She had begun to pay attention.

"Before you even open your mouth, I can tell what you're going to say. At eleven thirty every morning and at five o'clock every afternoon I know you will soon be home. In a crowd of a hundred women, I can recognize your footsteps right away. And as far as you're concerned, aren't I just as predictable?"

She stopped knitting and looked at me pensively.

"So neither of us can give the other any surprise at all," I went on. "All we can do is give each other a little pleasure, but that kind of pleasure is available anywhere in town."

Now she began to speak. "I understand what you're saying."

"Are you sure?" I didn't know how to respond, so that was all I could think of to say.

"I understand," she repeated. Tears began to slither down her face. "You want to dump me," she said.

I didn't try to deny it. "That sounds so crude" was all I said.

"You want to dump me," she said again. More tears.

"That's not a nice way to put it," I said. "Let's think about all the things we have done together."

"Is this the last time?" she asked.

I dodged the question. "Where shall we begin?" I went on.

"Is this the last time?" she repeated.

"How about we start from that autumn, back in 1977?" I said. "We took that clattering bus all those twenty kilometers to find out if you were pregnant. What a wreck I was that day!"

"No, you weren't," she said.

"Don't try to make me feel better. I really was a wreck."

"No, you weren't," she repeated. "In all the time I've known you, there's just once you've been a wreck."

"When was that?"

"Now."

A History of Two People

1

In August 1930 a boy named Tan Bo and a girl named Orchid sat side by side on a step untouched by sunlight. Behind them stood a vermilion gate, its copper latch in the shape of a lion. Tan Bo, the young master of the family, and Orchid, a maidservant's daughter, often sat together in this spot, while the maidservant went to and fro, carrying out her various duties amid the repetitive drone of the matriarch's mutterings.

There on the step, in lowered voices, the children talked about their dreams.

In his, Tan Bo was often tormented by a need to urinate. He would search high and low for a chamber pot, for the one that lay next to his bed in his comfortable south-facing room had vanished into thin air, and nowhere could he find the vessel that would release him from discomfort. Finally, in desperation, he would dash out to the main street, where rickshaws raced back and forth and beggars shuffled past. Unable to hold out a moment longer, Tan Bo would pee into the gutter.

Then the dream faded away. The sky was a patch of gray in the window as dawn began to break. What in the dream had been a street was actually a wooden bed, and as he woke Tan Bo felt a damp patch on the sheet and smelled a warm odor. Eyes wide with confusion, the boy painstakingly replayed the scenes from his dream but was soon jolted into full consciousness, and his wetting of the bed filled him with shame. As a bright glare began to fill the window, he closed his eyes once more and fell into a deep sleep.

"How about you?"

The boy's inquiry was suffused with eagerness. Clearly he hoped that in her dream the girl would have had just the same experience.

But faced with this inquiry, she proved bashful, clamping her hands over her eyes as girls her age are wont to do.

"Did you do the same thing?" the boy persisted.

A long, dark alleyway lay before them, high gray walls on either side. In the cracks between the bricks the recent years had planted coy little bunches of grass that quietly swayed back and forth in the breeze.

"Tell me." The boy's tone became aggressive.

The girl blushed red with shame. Hanging her head, she related a similar sequence of events. In her dream she too was desperate to pee, and she too looked everywhere for a chamber pot.

"You peed in the street too?" The boy was excited.

But she shook her head. She always found the chamber pot in the end.

This discrepancy deeply embarrassed the boy. He looked up, and above the alley's narrow walls he saw clouds floating through the sky and sunshine bathing the uppermost bricks.

Why can she find the chamber pot, when I can't? he thought.

Jealousy burned like a flame in his heart.

"Was the bed wet when you woke up?" he asked.

She nodded.

So at least the ending was the same.

2

In November 1939, seventeen-year-old Tan Bo no longer sat with sixteen-year-old Orchid on the stone steps in front of the gate. Now he wore a black school uniform and held in his hand a collection of Lu Xun's short stories and a book of Hu Shi's poetry. He was always in good spirits as he went in and out of the family compound. Meanwhile Orchid had inherited her mother's position. Dressed in a floral smock, she busied herself with household tasks amid the endless mutterings of old Mrs. Tan.

They were bound to exchange words from time to time, of course.

Youth surged through Tan Bo's body, and sometimes he would stop Orchid in her tracks and with animated gestures expound to her some progressive idea. On such occasions Orchid would lower her head and say nothing—the days when they shared everything without hesitation were long past, after all. Or perhaps Orchid was beginning to set store by Tan Bo's status as the young gentleman of the house. But he, immersed in the spirit of equality and mutual love, was hardly likely to realize the distance that was quietly developing between them.

On the last day of November, Orchid was running her dust

cloth over the rosewood furniture. Tan Bo sat by the window, reading Tagore's lines about the stray birds of summer. Orchid did her utmost to clean the furniture without making a sound, as she glanced at Tan Bo in slight agitation. She hoped that the current silence would not be interrupted. But reading is tiring and Tan Bo was bound to say something once he closed the book.

As a seventeen-year-old, he often dreamt that he was traveling on an ocean vessel, rocking back and forth in the waves. In his waking hours a longing to leave home would seize him.

He began to tell her about the restlessness that now infected his dreams. "I want to go to Yan'an," he told her.

She gazed at him in bewilderment. Clearly Yan'an was a meaningless blank as far as she was concerned.

He had no plans to make her understand anything further— all he wanted to know was the dreams that she had been having. The habit formed in 1930 died hard.

She blushed hotly, just as she had nine years earlier. Then she related a somewhat similar dream. The difference was that she was not on board a passenger ship but sitting in a sedan chair carried by four men; on her feet were pretty cotton shoes. The sedan chair threaded its way through the many streets in town.

He gave a little smile. "Your dream is different from mine." He paused. "You want to get married, I can see."

By then the Japanese had occupied the town where they lived.

3

In April 1950, Tan Bo, director of a performance troupe in the People's Liberation Army, a leather belt at his waist and puttees on his legs, returned to the home that he had not visited for ten years. The nation was now liberated, and between careers Tan Bo came back to have a look.

Orchid was still living in his house, but she no longer was his mother's servant, for she had begun to enjoy an independent life. Two rooms in the house had been assigned to her as living quarters.

The sight of Tan Bo striding energetically into the house left a deep impression on Orchid. By this time she had several children and had lost the slender figure of yesteryear; the turn of her broad waist was enough to efface the beauty she had once possessed.

Orchid had dreamt that Tan Bo would return home in precisely the manner in which he did. So, early one afternoon, her husband having left for work, Orchid told Tan Bo the scene from her dream. "You came back just as I dreamt you would."

She was no longer bashful and coy, for she was a mother of several children, of course. As she described the scene, there was no hint of lingering emotion—her tone was as level and bland as if she were telling him that someone had left a bowl on the kitchen floor.

Tan Bo recalled a dream he had had on his way home.

Orchid had appeared in that dream—not the woman before him now, but the girl she had once been.

"I dreamt of you, too," Tan Bo said.

Seeing Orchid so coarse and dumpy, he saw no point in describing her former charm. Dreams of her would now vanish from his sleeping consciousness.

4

December 1972. Tan Bo returned home in deep despondency, for he had been labeled a counterrevolutionary. His mother had died and he had come back to handle the funeral.

By this time Orchid's children had grown up and gone their own ways. She was still without a formal occupation. When Tan Bo stepped in through the door, she was scrubbing plastic sheeting. This activity was her main source of income.

As he passed her in his tattered black padded jacket, he stopped for a moment and smiled at her awkwardly.

Seeing him, Orchid gave a little gasp of surprise.

Only then did he go on toward his room in relief. Before long, Orchid knocked on his door and asked, "Is there anything you need?"

Tan Bo looked at the tidy arrangement of the room and didn't know what to say.

Orchid had made it her business to inform him of his mother's death.

This time, neither of them had any dreams to share.

5

October 1985. Tan Bo, retired and living at home, spent the day sunning himself in the yard. It was autumn yet, but he was sensitive to cold.

Orchid, now a white-haired old lady, was still hale and hearty. Though surrounded and sometimes harried by a flock of grandchildren, she took their demands in stride and never wearied of their company, while still attending to her chores, inside and out.

She laid a basin of clothes on the concrete pavers and began to do the laundry.

Tan Bo had to squint as he watched the vigorous movements of her arms. Amid her loud scrubbing he recounted with foreboding a couple of dreams that he kept having. A bridge collapsed just as he was crossing it. And when he was walking by the house, a roof tile hurtled toward his head.

Orchid said nothing and just kept on washing the clothes.

"Do you ever have dreams like that?" Tan Bo asked.

Orchid shook her head. "No, I don't."

Summer Typhoon

CHAPTER ONE

1

Bai Shu emerged from the little house at the north end of the school compound to find himself under the somber summer sky of 1976. The sky appeared before him suddenly when he came out the door, and its resonant gray expanse took him by surprise. The valley of memory then began to reverberate with the glimmer of days gone by, although the moss that grew on its stony sides marked how swiftly that light had passed.

It was as though a glance glittering with life had suddenly died, for the sky darkened as the boy walked on and the scene ahead of him re-created in his mind a hazy image from years before: a wooden bed with peeling paint on which his father lay, his eyes open but unseeing, as old and worn out as the bed itself. That night, as the moonlight came and went, his footsteps echoed along Riverwater Street and a flute cast its melancholy tune in all directions.

Now, above the grass in the middle of the playing field,

countless scraps of paper—fragmentary vestiges of revolutionary slogans and big-character posters—were whirling about, while the dust on all sides was tossed into the air and blew toward the paper scraps, making them dart about like birds alarmed by the twang of a bowstring. He could hear, in the distance, his name being called, for news of the Tangshan earthquake had begun to spread. It was Gu Lin or Chen Gang who had hailed him; the two were sitting there where the paper scraps were flying, while other classmates lay sprawled on the grass in the bright sunshine. Their question had to do with the earthquake monitoring station that he and the physics teacher had set up in that little house. Standing next to the stunted fir tree, he heard the gentle swaying of its needle-covered branches and then the lilt of his own voice: "We detected the Tangshan earthquake three days ago."

This was greeted with roars of laughter, and he laughed too, saying to himself, Actually, it was I who detected it.

The physics teacher was absent when it happened. The monitor had been quiet ever since it was installed, but at that particular moment it suddenly indicated an abnormality. The physics teacher had not been there to see—it had been ages, in fact, since his last appearance at the monitoring station.

Bai Shu had not told Gu Lin and the others that he was the one who had detected the tremor, for he felt that he should not exclude the physics teacher. And so their mockery was not directed at him alone, but the physics teacher could not hear it.

Their laughter swirled in the wind like those countless paper scraps, but the paper continued to flutter over the grass long after the laughter subsided. With the sun gone the grass looked all the more lush and green and the dancing paper took on a strange beauty. As Bai Shu walked on, still thinking about the physics teacher, he noticed how the leaves on the trees were drooping under a heavy coat of dust.

It was I alone who detected the Tangshan earthquake. He was convinced of this.

When the monitor indicated there had been an event, he was seized with panic, and after he left the house it took him a while to realize he was running as fast as he possibly could. After passing many trees and scaling many steps, he saw the chemistry teacher and the Chinese teacher making faces at each other in the staff room and only a globe visible on the desk of the physics teacher. He stood in the doorway until the Chinese teacher barked, "What do you want?"

This left him all flustered. Later, when he tapped on the door of the physics teacher's house, he made a noise as slight as the sound of his own breath, fearful that the teacher would not have the patience to hear him out. The door stayed closed.

At that moment the physics teacher was standing next to a line of faucets not far away, carefully washing a gaudy pair of panties and a white bra. When Bai Shu bashfully arrived by his side, he gave a grunt of acknowledgment and continued his scrubbing. He listened to Bai Shu's report and nodded. "I understand."

Bai Shu was expecting a further reaction, but the teacher did not raise his head or look at him again. He stood there a long time before plucking up the courage to ask, "Should we report to Beijing?"

Only now did the teacher raise his head. "How come you're still here?" he asked.

Bai Shu looked at him helplessly. The teacher said nothing more and simply raised the panties to eye level as though to check whether any spot had escaped his attention. Sunshine illuminated the colorful underwear, and Bai Shu, noting how freely and deeply the light entered, felt a tremor of excitement.

"What did you say just now?" the teacher asked.

Bai Shu licked his lip. "Should we report to Beijing?"

"Report?" The teacher frowned. "How do we report? To whom?"

Bai Shu was embarrassed. In the face of the teacher's impatience, he did not know what to do.

"If by any chance it's wrong, who's going to take the blame?"

He didn't dare say anything more, but continued to stand there until the teacher said, "Off you go, now."

But later, when questioned by his classmates on the playing field, he told them, "We detected the Tangshan earthquake three days ago." He didn't say that he alone had detected it.

"So why aren't you reporting it to Beijing?" They burst into laughter.

The physics teacher's comment was right on the mark. How to report? And to whom?

The scraps of paper continued to flutter. For some unknown reason, the monitor had suddenly stopped working. At first Bai Shu thought it was a power outage, but the dim yellow light of that 25-watt bulb was still shining. There must have been some malfunction in the instrument. He could not decide: Should he try to investigate this himself? Later he left the little house at the north end.

Now the paper scraps on the ground flew into the air far behind him. He walked out the school gate and followed the perimeter wall, toward the physics teacher's home.

The door to the teacher's house was painted light yellow, a

choice his wife had made, for another home she'd known had a door that same color. As Bai Shu knocked, he could faintly hear someone singing inside, and in his mind he pictured the ripples that used to spread across a pond in the early morning, agitating the strands of waterweed that floated on its surface.

The physics teacher's wife stood in the doorway. It was dark inside the house, but her figure was luminous, for with the light from outside shining on her she glowed like a lamp. Bright eyes looked at him, and then her bright lips began to move. "You're Bai Shu?"

He nodded. He saw how her left hand leaned against the doorframe, four fingers bent as though stuck there, one finger invisible.

"He's not home. He went out," she said.

Bai Shu's hand fumbled around on his leg.

"Come in," she said.

Bai Shu shook his head.

The laugh of the physics teacher's wife spilled out of an open book, and he heard the sound of an organ slowly rise from the classroom downstairs. In the songs that she sang in her music classes there was the same laughter as now. At one such moment the tree leaves stretched toward him through the open window, but he was forced to leave them and move toward the blackboard, where the physics teacher handed him a piece of chalk. As he stood there in front of the class, the organ downstairs seemed to strike a desolate note.

"You can't just stand there," she said with a smile.

It was always at that moment, when the organ music floated up from downstairs and the leaves outside the window reached toward him, that he was forced to abandon them both. He turned to leave, saying, "I'll go and look for him."

As he followed the perimeter wall, he sensed that she was still standing in the doorway, her eyes pinned on his figure. This thought made him walk with a swagger.

As he left the blackboard and returned to his seat, Gu Lin and the others burst out laughing.

The monitor broke down this morning—that was something Gu Lin and the others did not know, otherwise they would burst out laughing once more.

Having walked the full length of the wall, he had returned now to the main gate, and there he ran into the physics teacher on his way back from town. On hearing Bai Shu's report, the teacher nodded curtly. "I understand."

Bai Shu followed him. "Are you going to take a look?"

"All right," the physics teacher said. But he continued to walk toward his house.

"How about you go now?" Bai Shu persisted.

"All right, I'll go now."

The teacher walked a fair distance before he realized Bai Shu was still following him. He came to a halt. "Go on home," he said.

Bai Shu stood there watching as the teacher walked toward his house. The teacher didn't need to knock—all he needed to do was fish the key out of his pocket and he could enter, enter through the door that her hand had just touched. Because there was no light on inside, his wife stood shining in the doorway. She wore a black dress that came from a lively, bustling city.

He could see that the physics teacher was distracted as he handed him the chalk. The organ music from downstairs was wafting between them, and once more that lovely pond on the west side of town appeared in his mind's eye, along with the shrubs and trees that sheltered it. The organ continued to play its haunting tune. But he didn't know what he was supposed to do when he got to the blackboard. He and the teacher were equally bemused as the music rose and fell and the tree leaves swayed from side to side. He turned round and gazed inquiringly at the physics teacher, who had forgotten the task he had planned to assign. The two of them stood there looking at each other, until Gu Lin and the others started chuckling. "Go back to your seat," the teacher said.

His classmates hooted.

2

The physics teacher sat in a chair, his feet scuffing the floor restlessly. "It's bedlam out on the streets now."

She stuck her hand out the window, and the breeze blew the curtain toward her face. *A brown cow passed by, mooing as it went.* A long time ago, an expanse of rapeseed blossom had glittered in the sunlight and a white lamb had come trotting down from the distant grassy slopes. She closed the window. She had never paid another visit to her grandmother in the countryside. Now the light was on inside the apartment.

He turned to look at her and through the window beyond saw that the sky was murky. "The old guy who sells soy sauce—the one who lives opposite the west wharf—saw a pack of rats early this morning, all in a tidy line as they crossed the street, each gripping between its teeth the tail of the one in front. He said there were at least fifty of them, crossing the street in an orderly way, without the slightest panic. A driver from the machine plant saw them too. His truck didn't run them over—somehow that whole long procession managed to pass under his wheels."

She was in the kitchen now and he heard rice being poured into the pot. "That's what the old guy said?" she asked.

"No, not him. Someone else."

Water splashed into the pot.

"I always wonder how credible these rumors are," she said.

Her fingers stirred the pot and the water was dumped out.

"But everyone in the street is saying the same thing."

More water in the pot. "All it takes is for one person to say so, and everyone follows suit."

She knocked over a broom as she moved around in the kitchen, and then he heard her light the briquette stove.

"Last night there was a well south of here that seethed for two whole hours," he went on.

She came out of the kitchen. "That's just another rumor."

"But lots of people went to see, and they all confirmed it."

"Still just rumor."

He said nothing and simply put his hand to his forehead. She went over to the window. Even before the onset of night, the sky was already a leaden gray. Outside, a hen was stretching its wings and chasing something. She closed the curtains.

"Did you hear chickens and dogs last night?" he asked.

"No." She shook her head.

"Neither did I," he said. "But everyone else heard them— they were making a racket the whole night, apparently. We're the only ones who didn't hear, so we've got to believe them."

"Maybe they should believe *us*."

He got up from his chair. "Why do you never believe other people?"

"Is it heroes who create history? Or is it the masses who create history?" The politics teacher had asked.

"The masses create history."

"Who are the masses? Cai Tianyi."

"The masses are the entire working people."

"Sit down. How about the heroes? Wang Zhong."

"'Heroes' means slave-owners, capitalists, the exploiting classes."

On that day, the news of her grandmother's death in the countryside was still making its way toward her.

3

For some time now, reports had been circulating that an earthquake was imminent. Zhong Qimin sat by the window, his right hand on the windowsill, his left hand holding a flute. His eyes skimmed over the open lot before him, and through the leaves of the distant elm trees he looked for the sky. He could dimly make out a pale strip of light, bent like a worm. All at once its glow split into two pieces, and then the brightness at the two ends shrank until the light disappeared. But the sky kept on drifting just as calmly as before.

Wu Quan came back from the street with worrying news. "There's going to be an earthquake any moment. That's what the loudspeakers are saying."

Wu Quan's wife was standing at the doorway. For a pregnant woman, she had an unusually pale complexion. She watched in alarm as her husband walked toward her. He came up to her and said a few words, and she turned her ponderous body and went into the house. Wu Quan switched his attention to the anxious neighbors. "There's going to be an earthquake. The next county over made the announcement last night, but only now are they telling us here."

His wife emerged and slipped a roll of banknotes into his hand. "Be sure to collect all the valuables," he muttered.

He stuffed the money into his pocket and marched toward the street, crying at the top of his voice, "Earthquake's coming!"

As his shout receded into the distance, Zhong Qimin gave a sigh of relief, happy to see him go. A few people remained on the vacant lot, talking quietly.

"Earthquakes most often strike at night," Wang Hongsheng said.

"Usually when people are sound asleep," Lin Gang added.

"Earthquakes seem to prefer places where there are lots of people."

"Yeah, if there's nobody around, an earthquake is pointless."

"Wang Hongsheng!" an angry voice called.

Lin Gang gave Wang Hongsheng a push. "You're wanted."

Wang Hongsheng turned in the direction of the caller.

"Get back here! Help me figure out what to do."

Wang Hongsheng, looking bored, answered the summons. The others stood for a little while longer before they too dispersed. Now Li Ying appeared in the doorway, a woeful look on her face. "How come my husband's not back yet?"

Zhong Qimin picked up his flute and put it to his lips. One eye on the plaintive Li Ying, he began to play. *It was as though a strip of water, broad but thin, hovered in the sky. There were trees moving in the fields, their limbs emitting a soughing moan. When the river steamer left Wanxian, the night was deep, the massed mountains on both banks rising*

and falling like waves in the moonlight, their summits glisten-
ing. In the silence of night the river flowed, and the wind that
blew across the river had no place to go, so it arrived with a
wail and left with a wail as well.

With the rumors that an earthquake was on its way, his
window had lost its former calm. Everyone seemed to have
moved their beds closer to their doors, and he was constantly
hearing the noise of furniture being shifted around, tables and
beds driven this way and that like beasts of burden. As night
fell, the doors stayed open, and when sunlight shone in the
next morning he got vague and partial glimpses of people in
sleeping posture, and thus dawn's calm was silently shattered.

As the sun rose, an expanse of light grew freely in the crystal-
clear waters and the azure sea sang as it flowed past the bow to
mark a happy dawn. But later, sailboats began to appear in the
far distance, their sails stuck into the ocean surface like dilapi-
dated feathers, rocking back and forth in loneliness. That's the
heartbreak a vagabond feels as he follows his endless trail.

Li Ying's husband came back from town, bringing still
more alarming news. "Everyone's buying bamboos and plastic sheeting."

Zhong Qimin laid the flute on his right arm and watched as
Li Ying's husband walked toward his front door. Well, at least
he doesn't look so threatening, he said to himself.

"They've rigged up lots of shelters in the courtyard of the
County Revolutionary Committee," Li Ying's husband was
telling people, "and the school has put up shelters on the
playing field too. Nobody dares stay inside anymore—they
say there's going to be an earthquake tonight."

Li Ying came out of her house. "Where the hell have you
been?" she yelled.

On the streets everyone was rushing to buy bamboo and plastic rain sheeting. The window, tranquil for a while just now, was thrown into disturbance once more.

The inns where he had stayed had been on busy streets, and it was always impossible to gain a respite from all the noise. Clamor and din lacked the harmony and beauty that he craved, trumpeting and roaring for their own narrow purposes. If people just had a common goal, Zhong Qimin thought, then every little corner could give birth to music.

Wu Quan returned once more, this time heavily laden. "Better get over there!" he yelled as he unloaded bamboo and plastic sheeting from his cart. "Everyone's buying this stuff."

But the courtyard was already empty of menfolk, for they had rushed off to the shops a few minutes earlier, so his announcement did not elicit much of a reaction. Only a woman's voice rang out—it sounded like Wang Hongsheng's wife. "Why didn't you say so earlier?"

Wu Quan pretended not to hear this. His wife was now in the doorway, seemingly not daring to look in the direction of the noise. She took a few steps toward her husband, offering to give him a hand, but he said, "Leave it." So she stood where she was and watched with bowed head as he measured the ground with his foot.

"Let's put it here," he said. "That way, we won't get crushed if the house collapses."

She looked around. "I wonder if it's too much in the middle?" she murmured.

"It has to be here," he said.

The woman who had spoken earlier spoke up once more. "You can't put up a shelter there!"

Wu Quan again feigned deafness. He stood on a chair and stuck a bamboo pole into the earth.

"Hey, did you hear me?"

Wu Quan got down off the chair and picked up another bamboo pole.

"The guy has no shame." It was another female voice. "You ought to leave room for others."

"Wu Quan!" A woman's voice once more. "You've got to leave space for others."

It was all women talking, Zhong Qimin thought. Like shards of broken glass. He pressed the flute to his lips. *Sometimes music can conquer all before it. Late one night he had stood in a little alley that kept turning this way and that. The silence there was different from that of the vast grasslands or the high peaks—it was a hidden treasure that needed to be savored with care. When he resumed his wanderings, the alley kept turning corners and it was as though his walking was part of an incessant repetition, or an infinite simplicity.*

Now it was women's voices no longer. The air quivered with the cries of Wang Hongsheng, Lin Gang, and the others. They hadn't taken long.

"If you're reasonable, we'll be reasonable too. If you're not going to be reasonable, you can't expect us to be reasonable, either." Wang Hongsheng's voice carried loud and clear.

Lin Gang prepared to dismantle the shelter that Wu Quan had partially assembled. Wang Hongsheng restrained him. "Don't take it down yet. Wait till he's got it all up."

Li Ying was calling her son now. "Xingxing!"

"That kid keeps disappearing."

"Xingxing!" she called again.

Music can reign supreme. He had seen photographs of the moon's surface. In that harsh and desolate landscape there are no trees and no rivers, and no animal stirs. Everything is illuminated by a cold light, a light that is dark and sharp. It roams quietly among the coarse, untidy rocks. It's a world without a voice, a place where music should make its home.

A fresh-faced young boy was now sitting by his feet—he didn't know when he'd come in. The boy, target of the cries that could still be heard outside, sat quietly with a finger in his mouth, watching Zhong Qimin with a calm and artless gaze.

He felt he should play a tune that a child would like.

4

A couple of days earlier, the monitor had started working once more. The reason for the breakdown was simple: one of the lines going into the ground had snapped. Bai Shu had discovered the break near a tree on the west side of the sports field.

There, where twenty-four hours earlier scraps of paper were flying, a different spectacle could now be seen. Practically all the teachers in the school were milling around and makeshift earthquake shelters were beginning to appear.

In a yellowing book that had lost its cover, one could find a description of a campground: on a grassy slope, beneath snow-capped mountains, a dressing station for Allied casualties had been set up, and pretty nurses were walking to and fro among the tents.

The physics teacher had erected the frame for a shelter

and now was laying plastic sheeting on top. Off to one side the Chinese teacher said, "It's a bit too low."

"Safer this way," the physics teacher replied.

His shelter lay close to the road and leaned against a sturdy tree whose branches spread out above the tent. "They'll help block flying tiles," the physics teacher explained.

Bai Shu stood nearby. He looked in befuddlement at the spectacle before him. *Under a blue sky, the snow on the peaks was dazzling*—that was how he remembered the scene in the book, and he was baffled by the reality that had so suddenly taken shape. He did not move an inch, even after the Chinese teacher left. The physics teacher was busy with the plastic sheeting, so Bai Shu waited for him to finish and made his approach only when the teacher started walking around the tent to inspect his handiwork.

There was nothing wrong with the monitor, he told the physics teacher—it was just that a wire had been severed. He pointed to the spot. "Over there by the tree."

The physics teacher was surprised to see him. "Why have you not gone home yet?" he said.

He just stood there. "There is no abnormal activity on the monitor."

"Go on home," the physics teacher said. He continued to inspect the tent, before adding, "Don't come back here again."

Bai Shu stuck his hand in the pocket where he kept the key that opened the door to the little house at the north end. When the teacher told him not to come back, he interpreted this to mean: he wants the key back.

But the teacher said nothing about a key; he said only, "How come you're still here?"

As Bai Shu headed toward the main gate, he saw the physics teacher's wife coming his way along the perimeter wall. She was carrying heavy loads in both hands and her body was leaning to the right as the wind blew her black dress to the left.

Just then he heard the loudspeakers broadcasting the news that an earthquake was imminent. But the monitor had given no such signal. He watched as the physics teacher's wife trudged toward him. He felt sure that the broadcast had got things wrong. The teacher's wife was getting closer and closer. The loudspeakers were broadcasting an emergency speech delivered by the chairman of the County Revolutionary Committee. But the monitor reading was completely normal. The teacher's wife was now very near. She threw him a glance and went into the school.

In the street he ran into Gu Lin, Chen Gang, and the others, all in a state of high excitement. "There's going to be an earthquake at midnight tonight!" they cried. "We're not going to bother to go to bed."

He shook his head. "No way." The monitor was normal, he told them.

They burst out laughing. "Have you told Beijing?"

Then they walked on, shouting as they went, "Earthquake at midnight!"

Again he shook his head, again he said, "It's not going to happen."

But none of them heard.

It was nightfall by the time he got home. There was nobody there, and he knew his mother must have moved into one of the tents outside. He stood alone in the dark. The physics teacher's wife had walked slowly toward him, her body leaning to the right as the wind blew her dress to the left. He went downstairs.

He found his mother in the open lot outside. There were three tents there and his mother's was on the far right. She was making the bed and Wang Liqiang was picking up dishes. There was just the one bed, and he knew he'd be sharing it with his mother. He thought of that little house on the north side of the school—there was a bed there too. When setting it up, the physics teacher had told him, "In an emergency, there needs to be someone on duty."

Seeing him come in, his mother was a little embarrassed, and Wang Liqiang stopped picking up the dishes. "Ah, there you are," she said.

He nodded.

"I'll say goodbye," Wang Liqiang said. As he stepped out he added, "If you need anything, just call me."

Bai Shu's mother thanked Wang Liqiang politely.

Bai Shu thought: Actually, I know perfectly well what's going on between you two.

His father's funeral had been a wretched affair. Chang De, the man from the crematorium, had led the way, hauling the flatbed cart on which his father lay, covered by a white sheet. His mother shed no tears but raised her pale face toward the gloomy sky. He tramped along beside her as classmates on the way to school watched them from the sidewalk. It took them a long time to get where they were going.

CHAPTER TWO

1

Only the Tibetan sky can be such a deep, ethereal blue; it shrouds the peaks where no plants grow. The mountains in the foreground sported brown stripes, as though crawling with huge snakes. With the Kunlun mountains now behind, the bus had begun to enter the Tanggula range. A bank of clouds floated toward the baking sun and whittled away its light bit by bit, before finally arriving beneath the sun and challenging its authority. The plain suddenly darkened, as though night was about to fall. In the far distance he saw wild yaks ambling serenely, following their own trail through the tranquil colors of the high plateau.

Amid the drizzle, the flute brought to an end its final melody. As he sat by the window, Zhong Qimin pictured the tune he had just played shuttling through chinks in the rain and into the far distance, where it entered a sky he could not see, a sky in which dawn's rosy sunshine now fluttered. As the fields unrolled, the trees were the first to receive the sun's light. Over there, all the sounds of dawn were beginning to rise and merge with the sunshine, spreading everywhere in the pure air, without the least discordant note.

The pitter-patter of rain outside had persisted for days, just like the rumors of an imminent earthquake. Zhong Qimin gazed at the ramshackle shelters in the open lot, as rain beat down on the plastic sheeting under which the occupants were hidden. The concrete surface of the open lot was inches deep in water.

Lin Gang appeared in the one corner that was not yet occupied by tents. "Oh, that feels so good!" he shouted.

He turned around. "Wang Hongsheng! Hey, come over here."

"Where are you?" Wang Hongsheng's voice sounded as though it had been wrapped in a cotton sack. He must have stuck his head out of his tent as the rain pelted down.

No earthquake had arrived that night, when it was so confidently predicted. Instead the summer rains had come.

Wang Hongsheng and the others were now standing next to Lin Gang under a crowd of umbrellas, their heads pressed together. They lit cigarettes.

"It does feel good out here."

"Oh, it's unbearable in the tents."

"So incredibly stuffy."

"The worst thing is that plastic smell," said Wang Hongsheng.

"What's up with these cigarettes? They're so difficult to smoke."

"You might as well ask: What's up with this weather?"

It was a time of almost incessant drizzle. Zhong Qimin gazed at the trees in the distance that were shrouded in a damp mist. It was impossible to see the sky. *Rain concealed the blueness there ought to have been and blocked access to sunshine. That's what rain means: the sky is hidden.*

"Might there still be an earthquake?" Nobody had seen an

earthquake, and so nobody knew what ruins were like. *He had once visited the ruins of Karakhoja in Xinjiang. A town that once had prospered, after a millennium of baking in the hot sun and scouring by dust storms, is now a pile of ruins. He knew what ruins were. The vestiges of ancient houses and city walls could still be seen, but now they were half-buried in sand and glinting yellow in the sunlight. Once the sun set, the old town stood tall and chill in the moonlight, recalling the glory and doom of the past. And then music was born. So he knew what ruins were.*

"Zhong Qimin!" It was Lin Gang or maybe Wang Hongsheng calling him.

"He really wants to die a martyr." That was Wang Hongsheng.

By the time their laughter carried to his window, the rain had reduced it to shreds.

"I guess he thinks he's cool." This was Lin Gang.

The doors to their houses were all open, he noticed. Why didn't they go inside?

Li Ying was calling once again. "Xingxing!"

Umbrella open, she appeared next to Lin Gang and the others.

He didn't know when the child had arrived at his feet.

"That kid is always wandering off."

The child heard his mother's shout and pressed his finger to his lips.

"Xingxing!"

Xingxing's hair was wet through. Zhong Qimin bent down and dried the boy's face. The boy's shirt was soaked and his skin was turning white.

"Dawei!" Li Ying began to call her husband.

An answering call emerged from the tent.

"Come out of there!" Li Ying cried, sobbing. Again she shouted, "Xingxing!"

There was a patter of rain.

The boy's eyes glowed bright. He knew what he was looking forward to.

2

On the ground, water lapped to and fro, and the plastic sheeting flapped in the wind as the rain beat down with a dull, heavy rhythm. From time to time they heard snatches of the conversation between Wang Hongsheng and the others.

"Why don't you go stand outside for a bit too?" she said.

Wu Quan sat on the bed, his body bent, as sweat dribbled down his face. He shook his head.

She put her hand on his shirt. "Your clothes are all wet."

His hand was covered with pale wrinkles, as though it had been steeped in water for hours.

"Take your shirt off," she said.

But he just gazed at the water sloshing about. She reached out a hand to unfasten his buttons. "Don't do that," he said wearily. "Any kind of movement tires me out."

Damp, unruly hair concealed much of her face. She gripped the bed tightly, as though that was the only way to avoid tipping over. Her swollen belly made her lean slightly backward and her legs hung loose, the pale skin on her feet looking as though it had somehow detached from the underlying tissue, like a sheet of paper stuck clumsily on a wall and apt to be blown away at any moment.

Through the rain's constant patter the voices carried to them, along with the lilt of Zhong Qimin's flute and the wind's soughs. Occasionally the wind would make little forays into the tent, stirring movement in the stuffy atmosphere and opening up little cracks of comfortable space.

"Go on out for a bit," she repeated.

There was such a look of fatigue on her face that he couldn't bring himself to leave her on her own. He shook his head. "I don't feel like standing around with them."

The voices outside were still loud, but the flute had now fallen silent and the wind blew free and easy.

"I'll come out too," she said.

They crept out of the tent, unfurled the umbrella, and stood there, sucking in the fresh air.

"It's like opening a window when you get up in the morning," she said.

"Xingxing!"

Li Ying's shout sounded much louder now.

Xingxing emerged from the rain, his head sunk into his chest. He threw a glance at the window and Zhong Qimin waved his flute.

"Xingxing, where have you been all this time?" Li Ying sounded furious.

Her husband noticed that her legs were trembling. "Are you too tired for this?" he asked.

She shook her head.

"Let's go back."

"I'm not tired," she said.

"Let's go."

She turned around and took a couple of steps toward the tent, only to discover he was making no effort to follow her. "I really don't want to go back to the tent," he said with a frown. She smiled. "Then stay out here a bit longer."

"What I meant was—" He stopped. "Let's go over to our house. What I'm thinking is—" he went on. "We'll go to the house and sit for a bit—just in the doorway, I mean— and after that we'll go back." He threw a weary glance at the tent.

CHAPTER THREE

1

The monitor continued to show no sign of a pending earth- quake. In the morning the rain became patchy and the sky was no longer a heavy gray. Although black clouds still rolled across the sky, a reassuring pale light began faintly to reveal itself. The drizzle had persisted for three whole days. As he watched a few stray raindrops swirling through the air, he remained convinced that there wasn't going to be an earthquake.

In the streets, water was sloshing everywhere. That's what he had told Gu Lin and the others. The shelter occupied by the leader of the Workers' Propaganda Team stood in the middle of the sports field. *Under a blue sky, the snow on the peaks was dazzling.* But he could not tell the propaganda team leader that an earthquake wasn't going to happen; all he could say was, "The monitor is normal."

"The monitor?"

The team leader sat miserably inside the shelter, mopping the sweat off his bare arms.

"Damn it, why did I never hear about this monitor?"

He remained standing outside in the rain.

The team leader fixed his eyes on Bai Shu. "Does the thing work?" he asked suspiciously.

He had detected signs of the Tangshan earthquake three days before it happened, he answered.

The team leader took another long look at Bai Shu and shook his head. "How can you know ahead of time there's going to be such a big earthquake? That monitor is just for fooling around."

The physics teacher's shelter stood close to the path, and when the teacher's wife glanced Bai Shu's way as he walked in the rain, he felt he was crossing a forest bathed in sunlight. The monitor had detected no abnormalities: he wanted the physics teacher to know that. But the hand in his pocket stopped him; a key stopped him.

Now the drops of rain that hung in the air were becoming sparser, and a few sparrows flew across the street, their strident chirps anticipating the moment when sunlight would shine on the sodden earth. In the street he could hear people exchanging notes: "I gather there's not going to be an earthquake after all."

Bai Shu walked on amid the gossip.

"The next county over has already lifted its earthquake warning."

The monitor had not detected any abnormality. Bai Shu knew where he needed to go: it was all more pressing now.

When the stocky middle-aged man marched along the street, everyone eyed him with respect. Bai Shu was beneath his notice, but when the man saw Chen Gang he had asked, "How's your dad?"

"Do you know who that was?" Chen Gang had said to Bai Shu. "That's the chairman of the County Revolutionary Committee."

The scene in the County Revolutionary Committee compound was a duplicate of that on the school playing field. Tents of varying sizes had sprouted everywhere: still just like the campsite in the book, the one at the foot of the Alps. Bai Shu stood by the gate for some time and watched. Now that the rain had stopped, the residents stood outside their tents and pulled aside the plastic sheeting. "What a horrible smell!"

Bai Shu heard in their voices the exultation that only a sunny day could bring.

"Finally, that's the end of that."

"It was all a false alarm."

Several young people were struggling to peel back the roof of the biggest tent and lay it on the ground. The stocky man stood off to one side talking with others, but soon they hurried away and just one man in his thirties was left standing next to him. When the cover was turned over, a bright stream of water spilled down. The two men entered the now-roofless tent.

Bai Shu came closer, until he was within speaking distance. The official was sitting in a chair and rubbing his knees, while the younger man stood by a desk, telephone in hand. "Do we inform the broadcasting station?" he asked.

The committee chairman waved his hand in demurral.

"First let's touch base with . . ." Bai Shu could just make out the name of a neighboring county.

The other man began to dial. "Is that the long-distance desk? Please connect me with . . ."

"Who are you?" The chairman had finally noticed him.

"The monitor has detected no abnormalities." Bai Shu heard his words drifting shakily toward the chairman.

"What's that?"

"The monitoring—the earthquake monitor is normal."

"Earthquake monitor? Where did that come from?"

The phone rang and the man picked up. "Hello, is that . . . ?"

"Our school's earthquake monitor," Bai Shu said.

"Your school?"

"The county high school."

The man was speaking on the phone. "You've lifted the warning?" He put down the receiver. "They've lifted the warning too."

The chairman nodded. "They all have." He turned to Bai Shu. "What were you saying?"

"The monitor has been normal all along."

"At your school? You have an earthquake monitor?"

"That's right." Bai Shu nodded. "We detected the Tangshan earthquake."

"Well, I'll be darned!" A grin appeared on the chairman's face.

"The monitor has been normal. There's not going to be an earthquake." Bai Shu finally came out with the prediction he had made when talking to Gu Lin and the others.

"Ah." The chairman nodded his head. "I understand what you're saying. There'll be no earthquake?"

"No," Bai Shu said.

The chairman stood up and came toward Bai Shu. He proffered his right hand, but Bai Shu didn't understand what he meant, so he drew it back again. "You've performed a great service," he said. "I thank you on behalf of the people of the county." He turned to the other man. "Write his name down."

Later Bai Shu walked again along the street, where water still sloshed. By then the news that there would be no earthquake was spreading throughout the town. In the streets, people were carrying bedrolls and cooking equipment—the first detachment of residents to abandon their tents and head for home.

"Bai Shu!"

He saw Wang Ling sitting on the steps of the theater. He was soaked through, but he looked at Bai Shu with a big smile on his face.

"Did you hear?" Wang Ling said. "The earthquake's not going to happen."

He nodded. Then the loudspeakers began to crackle. "The neighboring counties have now lifted the earthquake warning. According to monitor Bai Shu of our county's monitoring station, there will be no earthquake in the near future. . . ."

"Bai Shu, they're talking about you!" Wang Ling yelled.

Bai Shu stood there, dumb, as the announcer's voice slowly faded away; then he walked along the steps and sat down next to Wang Ling. Drops of moisture were encroaching on the scene before him, and he reached out a hand to brush away the tears.

Wang Ling was shaking his arm. "Bai Shu, your name's in the news!"

The boy's excitement stirred him. "Wang Ling," he said, "how about you come to the monitoring station too?"

"Do you really mean it?"

The physics teacher's image suddenly came to mind, and Bai Shu felt uneasy about the words he had just blurted out, unsure whether the teacher would approve.

The physics teacher's tent was right next to the street, and passing it meant passing his wife's glance.

He had seen her standing beneath a tree. The leaves had partly blocked the sunlight, so it was dappled light that reached her body. He noticed how the shadows of the leaves shifted unhurriedly on her body. What happy shadows! "I'm hopeless," she was saying to the physical education instructor.

The PE instructor was standing next to the sandpit, inviting her in, like the sandpit itself.

By now she too should have heard the broadcast.

2

The drizzle, persistent for so long, at midday tapered off and then stopped completely. When Zhong Qimin sat by the window and gazed into the far distance, he saw scattered clouds marching rapidly across the sky. *He had once stretched out a hand to touch those scudding clouds; as he neared the peak, clouds as dark as smoke had billowed up from below and swept all before them. Those floating giants were actually just as fragile and ephemeral as smoke, and their dispersal was inevitable.*

On the open lot, Li Ying was once more calling Xingxing. It was always so easy for him to run away. Lin Gang was there too, throwing open the plastic sheet that covered his tent. "Time for some sunbathing!"

"Where's the sunshine?" Wang Hongsheng emerged from his tent, thinking Lin Gang was serious.

"Clouds are in the way," Lin Gang said. It was true. "Turn the sheet over," he shouted. "Get rid of that stink."

As the sheets were pulled back and dumped on the ground, the open lot began to look like a garbage dump. Wu Quan's wife stood inside a now uncovered shelter, and her swollen belly entered Zhong Qimin's line of vision.

"Xingxing!" Li Ying was calling.

"Let him be," Wang Hongsheng said. "Give the boy a chance to play."

"But he's just a kid." Li Ying always wore a frown.

Music had fled from the scene. They were making as much din as the Japanese did that year they crossed the Marco Polo Bridge, and so music had quickly made itself scarce. As Zhong Qimin rose from his chair, a fresh breeze was blowing. He wished he could insinuate himself into the breeze and roam across the endless fields.

As Zhong Qimin went out, Dawei came back from town. "There's not going to be an earthquake," he said, and added still more encouraging news. "Everyone's moving back into their homes."

"What about Xingxing?" Li Ying shouted.

"How would I know?"

"That's right—all you know is fooling around."

"All you can do is yell."

It was going to be a long row. Zhong Qimin stepped into the street. *Quarrels between men and women are the stu-*

pidest noise in the world. Water was still eddying, and as he advanced he felt flowers of foam blossoming and withering at his feet.

He saw people plodding along with bedrolls on their shoulders and cooking equipment in their hands, under a sky where black clouds scudded; children were following behind. They all seemed to be in high spirits, but high spirits could hardly conceal their bedraggled appearance. Wang Hongsheng and the others meanwhile were retrieving their bedrolls and cooking equipment from the tents and taking them home.

The earthquake was not going to happen.

Zhong Qimin felt someone tugging at the hem of his shirt. Xingxing was standing next to him, his pant legs and shirtsleeves rolled up high—a look he was proud of.

"There's no one there," Xingxing told him.

The boy seemed to be pointing toward a line of plane trees, and once an old man had passed, there really was no one else.

Xingxing headed off in that direction, his hand still clutching Zhong Qimin's shirt, so he had no choice but to follow. When they reached the trees, the boy released his grip, walked forward a few steps, and pushed open the door to a house. "Nobody inside."

It was utter darkness inside. Zhong Qimin knew where the boy wanted to take him. "I just came out of my house," he said.

The boy paid no heed and went on in. *Children are tyrants.* Zhong Qimin followed. The boy was going up the stairs, stairs as long and winding as an alley. Later a little light filtered down, and then the stairs ended. They made a right turn, the boy leading once more. A small hand pushed open a large door and then it was the same small hand that closed the door. He saw some furniture and a bed; the curtains were open. Now the boy was over by the windowsill and there was a squeak of curtains being drawn. He had to extend to his fullest height to reach them, and his legs trembled from standing on tiptoe. More squeaks as the curtains shifted reluctantly.

One more squeak, and the two curtains were now almost touching. The boy turned and looked at him, and the light that slipped through the crack between the curtains drifted over his hair. The boy leaned against the wall and slipped down until he was sitting on the floor. He listened carefully, then said, "Outside is quiet now."

The boy put his hands on his knees and gazed at him silently, his eyes gleaming. Zhong Qimin knew what was expected, so he brought a chair over and sat down. First he straightened his shirt, then he raised his hands and made the motions of playing an instrument. Finally came the contrite apology: "I didn't bring the flute."

The boy looked at him reproachfully. He put a hand against the wall and pushed himself upright, then turned away and peered over the windowsill once more. When he glanced back, his face was framed by light. "I thought you had it with you."

"Let's guess a riddle," Zhong Qimin said.

"What's the riddle?" The boy's despondency began to lift.

"Whose house is this?"

Not much of a riddle.

The boy looked away again, his eyes ranging over the sky and leaves and electric wires outside the building. Then he turned back, eyes glowing. "It's Chen Wei's."

"Who's Chen Wei?"

The boy, confused, shook his head. "I don't know."

"That's fine," Zhong Qimin said. "Let's play something different. Come over here and stand in front of this chest of drawers. Let me think—how about you open the third drawer?"

The boy pulled it open.

"What's inside?"

The boy stuck practically his whole top half into the drawer, then brought out a few sheets of paper and a pair of scissors.

"Great, give them to me."

The boy handed them over.

"I'll make you a ship, or a plane."

"I don't want a ship or a plane."

"What *do* you want?"

"I want glasses."

"Glasses?" Zhong Qimin raised his head and threw the boy a glance, then got to work making paper glasses. "What do you want glasses for?"

"To wear here." The boy pointed at his eyes.

"To wear on your mouth?"

"No, to wear here."

"Around your neck?"

"No, to wear here."

"Got it." Zhong Qimin finished his creation and put it on the boy. "Here you go." The paper covered the boy's eyes.

"I can't see anything."

"How could you?" Zhong Qimin said. "Take the glasses off, carefully. . . . If you look right, what do you see?"

"Chest."

"What else?"

"Table."

"If you look left, what do you see?"

"Bed."

"What about straight ahead?"

"I see you."

"If I move away, what do you see?"

"Chair."

"Very good, now put the glasses on again."

The boy put them on again.

"If you look right, what do you see?"

"Chest and table."

"And to the left?"

"A bed."

"And in front?"

"You and a chair?"

"Can you see now?" Zhong Qimin asked.

"Yes, I can," the boy said.

The boy began to move around the room cautiously. It was indeed quiet here. A long sliver of light hung from the window. *He had once walked alone in a forest, and with the branches interlocking above his head and the leaves covering one another, the sky had looked tattered and disjointed.* The boy seemed to have opened the door—he could see it too. *Sunlight had flitted about, hopping from one leaf to another.* The boy was going downstairs, hopping from one step to the next. *From beneath his feet had come the faint sound of leaves crackling, as soft as freshly tilled earth.*

Zhong Qimin felt someone shaking his chair from behind. Xingxing had not gone downstairs, after all. But when he turned around, he did not see the boy. The chair kept shaking. He stood up and went over to the window, to find the curtains quivering. Pulling them open, he could see people in the streets standing paralyzed with fear. They were maybe the last people to evacuate from the tents, bedrolls and cooking equipment still in their hands. He opened the window and everything outside was still—the same calm that you find in the ancient city of Gaochang.

Now there were people shouting: "Earthquake!"

Reports about earthquakes had proliferated like snowflakes for many days, but what came in the end was a silence like that of the desert near Turfan.

In the street, people began to run, in panic and desperation. The silence of a moment earlier was shattered, and he heard a chaotic medley of sounds torn through with sobs and wails. Zhong Qimin left the window and moved toward the door. He put out his hand and touched the chair: it was no longer shaking. But the world outside was seething with noise. *That's what an earthquake is like: it gives you a momentary serenity, and then everything turns to clamor once more. An earthquake won't give you ruins so easily, it won't give you lasting peace.*

When Zhong Qimin came out onto the street, he found a long line of people walking along with bedrolls and cooking equipment on their backs. Even before the first evacuation had ended, a second exodus had started. They were returning to the earthquake shelters. The street was crowded with the sounds of people, just as alarmed and lost as before.

As dusk arrived, Zhong Qimin sat at his window. Someone came back from town with the latest news: "The broadcast said that was a foreshock, and the main shock will follow. Everyone must be on high alert."

CHAPTER FOUR

1

The straw mat on the bed was completely soaked through. When it first got wet, it still gave off a warm, grassy scent, but now it was dotted with white spots of mold. As she slowly rubbed them off, it felt as if her fingers were touching sticky specks of rotting food.

The constant surge of floodwater moderated the rise in temperature inside the tents. The water underfoot divided into two streams and flowed away, and in the no-man's-land where the two streams met, froth leapt gaily in all directions. As the water drained, it created crystalline patterns that shone like wisps of light, and in the water's churning there lingered a cool freshness like that which covers the earth at the dawn of an early autumn day.

Queasy for many days now, she slipped both hands inside her pants to put some space between her skin and her sodden clothes. Wu Quan had thrown up several times, and, each time, his hands trembled alarmingly as he bent down, clutching his hips to avoid toppling over. His mouth gaped emptily, for he now vomited only sound and saliva. It was as though a chisel were chipping away at his throat, so grating was the noise. Though racked by nausea, she had to put up with it, for if she were to actually be sick, Wu Quan would start gagging all the more fiercely.

She saw three centipedes wriggling on the tarp opposite, each crawling in a different direction. She seemed to make out the silky hairs on their heads. They stretched and then contracted as they crawled, leaving three bright trails on the tarp, each a series of arcs.

"We'd be better off dead!" It was the sound of Lin Gang shouting outside. He made a loud splash as he stormed out of the shelter and put his foot in a puddle. Then there was the sound of a door closing as he went inside his house.

"Lin Gang!" Wang Hongsheng emerged from another shelter.

"I just want to die!" Lin Gang cried from inside.

She turned to look at her husband. Wu Quan had raised his head as though anticipating further cries, but all he heard was the clamor of wind and rain and the insistent drip of water on the tarps. So he bowed his head once more.

"Wang Hongsheng!" A woman's sharp voice.

Her husband's bare chest, she now saw, was covered with red spots. The spots ascended his body, scaled his neck, and climbed his face. As evening arrived, she heard the hum of mosquitoes. They flew into the shelter as the rain poured down and made more noise than she could ever have imagined.

"Stay in the shelter!" It was Wang Hongsheng's voice.

"Why should I?" His wife.

"It's for your own good."

"I can't take it anymore, either." She began to sob. "Why did you leave me and go back to the house by yourself?"

"It's for your own good!" He'd begun to yell.

"Get out of the way." More yelling. Maybe he was dragging her back.

She heard a sharp whack—he must have clipped her over the ear, she thought.

"So that's the way you want it!" There was wailing and shouting and more hitting.

She turned and saw her husband again raising his head.

The loud slam of a door, and then a crash as it was kicked.

"I don't want to go on living—"

Much crying. Sobs and wails pierced the darkness. The woman seemed to have collapsed on the floor. Fierce bangs on the door.

Listening closely, she guessed the woman was butting the door with her head.

"I—don't—want—to—go—on—living."

The crying suddenly became staccato. "You—bastard!" The wife was cursing her husband.

"Wang Hongsheng, open the door!" Someone else was shouting.

The crying grew fitful; it was interspersed with spatters of rain. She heard a door being thrown open and guessed that Wang Hongsheng must be standing in the doorway.

Flute music issued from Zhong Qimin's window. Its notes lingered long, as though blown along a river by the morning breeze. That fool was constantly playing his flute. "Fool" was the label conferred on him by Wang Hongsheng and the others. Lin Gang had been standing underneath his window one day, and Wang Hongsheng was chuckling off to one side. "Fool!" Lin Gang called, and to their delight Zhong Qimin poked his head out.

"Dawei," Li Ying called, "have you seen Xingxing?"

Dawei seemed to have been gone a long time, and his answer was weary. "I couldn't find him."

Li Ying sobbed despairingly. "What on earth do we do?"

"Somebody saw him a couple of days ago." Dawei's voice

was low and feeble. "They said he had a piece of paper over his eyes."

The flute music broke off.

How could it stop? These past three years, it had been such a regular part of life. Like the rain, it constantly twined around them. On those clear, mild evenings, Wu Quan's snores would drift out the open windows while the strains of Zhong Qimin's flute drifted in. She had slept so soundly then, at ease between these two familiar sounds.

"He was walking down the street with paper over his face," Dawei said.

"What are we going to do?" Li Ying sobbed weakly.

She turned to find her husband, head bowed, scraping dead skin off his hands. The skin had crinkled from being wet so long, and he was scraping away the pale top layer, one shred after another. He had done this several times already and once he got started there was no stopping: his hands were a terrible sight. She looked at her own dropsied hands: they too looked as though they had been soaked overlong in water, but she had not scraped off the dead skin. If she had, her hands would be just like his.

A house centipede was inching its way along the bed frame toward her husband's leg, its plump midriff curving in a smooth, supple way with each forward movement. It leaned its head against his leg, then climbed on top, crawling along the leg in a series of stretches and contractions. A shiny trail extended along the bed frame and onto his leg, connecting the two.

"A centipede," she called softly.

Wu Quan lifted his head blankly and looked at her.

"Centipede," she said again, pointing at his left leg.

He stretched out his hand and tried to catch the centipede between his fingers, but it was too slippery. He changed his mind, flicking it away with his forefinger. The centipede rolled into a ball and fell off his leg, and soon it was swept away by the rainwater.

He stopped scraping his skin. "I want to go back to our house," he said.

She looked at him. "Me too."

"You can't." He shook his head.

"No," she persisted. "I want to be with you."

"You can't," he objected. "It's too dangerous."

"That's why I want to be with you."

"No."

"I want to go there." Her tone was mild.

"You need to think of the child." He pointed at her swollen belly.

She said nothing more and watched as he wearily pulled himself up, put one foot into the water, ducked his head, and stepped outside. He stood there for a moment as the rain fell on his upturned face, and his eyes narrowed to slits. Then she heard splashes receding into the distance.

Zhong Qimin's flute could now be heard once more. His piping tune, long and sinuous as the wind itself, blew in through the window as Wu Quan entered his house. He took care not to lie down in bed, for he was really too tired—just talking was enough to exhaust him.

"Dawei, go and look one more time, will you?" Li Ying begged, with tears in her eyes.

The best thing to do was to move a chair to the doorway and sit there. He could manage that.

Dawei tramped off through the rainwater.

There was the sound of a door opening, and then Lin Gang's despondent voice. "It's unbearable indoors, too."

Lin Gang splashed his way back toward the shelters.

Wu Quan, sitting in his house, found it equally unbearable. Tension seized him: it felt as though the corners of the room were shaking.

Wu Quan reappeared at the entrance to the shelter and his pallid face turned toward hers. "It's shaking again."

2

Late at night the trill of Zhong Qimin's flute drifted in the rain, like a sail wending its way across an ocean, floating in the dark distance. Rain continued to beat upon the tarps, and the sound of lapping water rose up from the ground as wind whistled through. Swarms of mosquitoes flew around inside the shelter. They landed on Wu Quan's bare chest, then took flight again in a jumble of legs and wings, and in their humming he detected sounds of panic and disarray. His wife was already asleep, her breathing like ripples on the surface of a lake, pulsing off into the far distance—or that's what it would have been like in the past, on those rainless evenings when moonlight shone through the window. Now the din of mosquitoes drowned out his wife's breathing. The straw mat underneath him gave off a whiff of warm, decaying damp-ness, *the furry odor of rice that has gone bad, different from the odor of rotten fruit or putrid meat. When rice goes bad, it takes on a color between blue and yellow.*

When he sat up in bed, his wife did not react. There was a flurry of mosquitoes as they vacated his body with a tumultuous hum. He put his foot into the flowing water and a chill rose quickly all the way up to his chest. He gave a shiver.

When they fished He Yongming out of the river in the middle of a sweltering summer day, his body was chalk-white and swollen. After they laid him in the shade of a tree, a swarm of mosquitoes flew over from the shrubs to stake their claim, and soon countless spots appeared on his distended body. When someone approached, the mosquitoes hastily abandoned the corpse and flew around in confusion, just like now.

I want to go back to my house.

He sat like that for a while, longing to be home. It felt as though a mosquito had flown into his mouth just as he was taking a breath, and he wanted to spit it out, but it was too difficult. When he stood up, he knocked against the tarp, and it was cool to the touch. The rain fell on his bare shoulders, refreshing but also a little chilly. He saw someone standing in the rain smoking. He seemed to be holding an umbrella, and the cigarette blinked on and off. There was no light in Zhong Qimin's window, but flute notes drifted outside like specters. Rain fell fiercely.

I want to go back home.

He took a step toward his house. The door was open and inside was dark—darker even than other places. But there was nothing to stop him from going there, although the water lapped around his feet, obstructing his passage, and it was heavy going.

I'm home now.

He stood in the doorway for a moment. One corner of the

room was in utter darkness and to his eyes looked completely bare. It had twisted and cracked in the earthquake, and now there was nothing there at all.

Why am I standing in the doorway?

He felt his way forward. A chair blocked his way and he pushed it aside and continued on. He groped and found the banisters that led toward the bed on the second floor. He followed the stairs up. It seemed as though something was about to happen; people outside had been talking about it for a long time. It seemed to be important, but what was it, exactly? How could he not remember what it was? Not long ago he used to know—and he had even talked about it. But now he couldn't remember at all. There were no more stairs, so no more need to raise his feet—that was really too much effort. The bed was on the north side, and this was the right way to get there. *Here's the bed, it sure feels hard. Now you can sit down, it feels soft when you do that, so let's get the shoes off and lie down. How come I can't get my shoes off? Oh, they're off already. It's all right now, you can lie down. How come there's no sound of water on the floor, could it be you just didn't hear it? Now I can hear it, the water lapping all around, and the wind is fierce, blowing the tarps so they shake back and forth. The rain is hitting the tarps, deedeedada—such a familiar sound.* A swarm of mosquitoes flew over, humming away. They landed on his chest and then flew off again. The mat underneath him channeled damp air toward his face. *The rotten smell is warm, the furry smell that develops after rice goes bad, different from the odor of rotting fruit or putrid meat. When rice goes bad it turns a color between blue and yellow. I want to go back home. My limbs can't move and my eyes won't open. I want to go home.*

3

In the early morning the raindrops grew sparse. Zhong Qimin sat by the window, listening to the sounds that came from nature. *The wind casually fluttered in the air, coming from the fields in the far distance, ruffling the surface of the three ponds it passed, shaking the tree leaves so they rustled incessantly. One morning he had heard a band of children quarreling in the distance, and the leaves swaying in the morning breeze had the same freshness as those children's voices. Children's cries and early morning: there's a connection there. Wind— nature's most sustained sound—blew in through the window.*

This kind of morning was not such an ordinary event. Reports of an impending earthquake had long been circulating, but then the rains had come, and after that a quiet morning like this—the kind of morning that rules out coughs and footsteps and the scratching of a broom on a concrete floor.

"He must have been in a total panic," Wang Hongsheng said. He gave a cough or two. "Jumping from the second floor shouldn't kill you."

"He must have jumped headfirst and hit his head on a flagstone."

They were always standing around and babbling away underneath the window. They would never understand that sound cannot be so casually squandered, because music would never be born amid such nonstop chatter—music would sooner flee. But at least their constant chatter was milder than the women's grating squabbles. Whenever they came on the scene, it was like a flock of sparrows and a flock of ducks passing at the same time, and their bickering was always remorseless and unending.

Dawei headed off toward the street in a dark raincoat. Three days earlier Xingxing had put on his paper glasses, then gone out and not come back. Dawei would now go off each morning, back hunched, and later he would return in just the same dejected state. Li Ying stood in the rain watching as he walked away. She did not open her umbrella but just let the rain fall. This morning she had suddenly stopped crying.

He saw Wu Quan's wife emerge from the open door of her house and waddle clumsily past his window.

"What's she up to?" Lin Gang asked.

"Looking for a man, maybe." It was Wang Hongsheng who answered.

They went on standing there.

Morning calm is always elusive. But one morning he had lain on the banks of the Daning River and in the silence all around he had heard with utter clarity the flow of the river, the sounds of nature.

When she returned, she was pushing a cart. She pushed it all the way to her front door and then she went inside. Her extra weight made her every movement look onerous, and when she came out again her strength faced an even sterner test, for now she was carrying someone in her arms. But somehow she could manage it. A couple of people went over to lend a hand, and together they put the person on the cart. She went back inside as the others stood around, and through the morning drizzle he could see that the man on the cart was Wu Quan. His face had lost all expression, and it was as though his features had been cobbled together with children's building blocks. When she came out, she covered Wu Quan with a white cloth, and then a tarp on top of that. Someone tried to push the cart, but she waved him away and began to push it herself. As it passed beneath his window, Wang Hongsheng and Lin Gang went over as though to offer help but again were waved away. Drops of rain fell on her upraised face and matted her hair. He had a clear view of her, and it made him think of a song called "Shall I Tell You What Is Heartbreak?" As she pushed the cart on toward the street, her body swayed awkwardly and her legs strained with effort because of the child she was carrying. Her unborn child was with her in the rain.

Before long a new child would appear in that courtyard, bracing himself against the wall and waddling as he walked, a bit like his mother now. The child would grow up quickly, until he was as big as Xingxing, when he too would sneak over and sit quietly at his feet as he played the flute.

As she went, she splashed water in all directions and the raincoat she was wearing was as bright as morning. Her walking was labored, yes, but it was not crude. A woman and a cart advanced through the boundless rain.

In a little town on the banks of the Fuchun River, he had glimpsed a solemn funeral procession. The line of wreaths was as long as the street, and thirty horns pointed to the sky, wailing long and loud, and weeping fluttered through the sky like a banner.

CHAPTER FIVE

1

Amid the rain, red fruit were gleaming and the grass was waving. That was the view from the window of the little house at the north end.

Down on street level, the water that had accumulated on the sides of the road was sloshing back and forth. Rain cast a shroud, disconnecting the red fruit from the grass at the north end of the playing field. The fruit gleamed beside the road that Bai Shu was walking along, its redness standing out in a scene otherwise dominated by darkness and rain.

Four days earlier, the street had undulated like a river when he and Wang Ling were sitting on the steps of the theater and the earthquake unleashed scenes of panic and alarm. He had rushed back to the little house in the northernmost corner, but the monitor had not shown any sign of abnormal activity. Later, as the rain grew heavier, Gu Lin and the others had accosted him.

It happened here, by the dying plane tree. His head had knocked against this very tree.

Gu Lin and the others had blocked his path. "Admit it." Gu Lin spoke in anger. "You've been making things up."

"No, I haven't."

"How about you repeat what you said, that there wouldn't be any earthquake?"

He said nothing.

"Are you going to say it?" He watched as the palm of Gu Lin's hand struck his face a heavy blow. Then his chest took a fist—the work of Chen Gang.

"We'll let you off if you just admit you were fabricating rumors," Chen Gang said.

"The monitor reading has been normal the whole time. I didn't make up any rumor."

For that he received a clip on the ear.

"Then say there's not going to be an earthquake," Gu Lin said.

"I'm not going to say that."

Gu Lin did his best to sweep his feet from under him, and he swayed back and forth but did not fall. Chen Gang pushed Gu Lin aside. "I'll teach him."

Chen Gang kicked him fiercely in the leg. When he fell on the ground, water splashed everywhere, and his head knocked against the plane tree.

At this spot four days earlier he had clambered up out of the water as Gu Lin and the others went off laughing raucously. He'd wanted to tell them that the monitor would definitely have detected the earthquake, it was just that he had not been in the little house at the time, and so he had no way of knowing in advance that the earthquake was coming. But he did not say that, and after Gu Lin and the others had gone some distance they turned around and waved their fists in his direction. He had not been there, and so he could not have said.

A tree leaf was stirring in the water on the street. The table in the monitoring station was covered with water droplets, like a tree leaf in the rain. For four days the monitor had detected no abnormal activity. Now he was walking toward the County Revolutionary Committee headquarters.

That stocky middle-aged man was cordial and friendly. He was different from Gu Lin and the others: he would believe what Bai Shu said.

He entered the County Revolutionary Committee compound, and there in the middle, among the many temporary shelters, was that biggest shelter of all. When the chairman walked through the streets he was regarded with awe by passersby, but to Bai Shu he was friendly and cordial.

He saw the chairman now: he was sitting on the bed and he looked exhausted. The man who had been at his side four days earlier was with him again, dialing the phone. Bai Shu stood at the entrance to the shelter. The chairman saw him but paid no attention, his eyes fixed on the phone.

He hesitated for some time before saying, "The monitor reading is normal."

The call went through, and the man talked into the receiver.

The chairman seemed to have recognized him, for he nodded. The other man finished talking on the phone and hung up. "Well?" the chairman asked brusquely.

The assistant shook his head. "They haven't lifted the warning, either."

He cursed under his breath. "Damn it, when is this going to end?" Only then did he ask, "What did you say?"

"For the last four days the monitor reading has been normal," he said.

"The monitor?" He looked at him for a long time, and finally said, "Very good, very good. You must definitely continue to monitor. This is important work."

He felt a few droplets in his eyes. "Gu Lin and the others accused me of making things up."

"That was unfair," the chairman said. "Go on back. I'll tell your teacher to criticize the classmates who accused you."

The physics teacher had said the monitor could predict earthquakes.

He was walking in the street once more, this time confident that he was believed. Then he realized he had forgotten a key point, that the monitor had definitely detected the tremor of four days earlier, but he had simply not been present at the time.

Tell him later, he said to himself.

The physics teacher's wife was sitting in the shelter; through the pouring rain he could see her watching him. They had spoken on a bright afternoon, but now the sports field was empty and desolate and he walked alone toward the main gate of the school.

"Is this your satchel?" Her voice had filled the field with flowers in bloom. The sight of her walking toward him was what had led him to forget the satchel.

"Bai Shu!"

Rain was spinning through the air. The shout had come from beneath the dripping eaves. Chen Gang was sitting in front of an ancient black door. "Have you seen Gu Lin and the others?"

Chen Gang sat on the doorsill, his body hunched.

Bai Shu shook his head. The slanting rain separated him from Chen Gang.

"Could there still be an earthquake?"

Bai Shu rubbed the raindrops off his face. "The monitor is normal," he said. He didn't say there wouldn't be an earthquake.

Chen Gang rubbed his face too. "I'm sick," he told Bai Shu.

A gust of wind blew, and Chen Gang shivered. "I have a fever."

"Better go back inside," Bai Shu said.

Chen Gang shook his head. "I'm not going back to the shelter, even if it kills me."

Bai Shu continued on his way. Chen Gang was sick, but the teacher would soon reprimand him. He couldn't blame them for what happened four days earlier. He shouldn't have told the committee chairman what they had done.

Wu Quan's wife appeared out of the rain, pushing a flatbed cart. Its wheels sent water spattering in all directions as they rolled along the street, and the wind made her raincoat flap wildly. As the cart passed, a gust of wind blew the shroud to one side, revealing Wu Quan's face, now eerily serene. The spark of life had died just as suddenly in Bai Shu's father's eyes, before a tranquil expression appeared on his face too. Wu Quan's wife struggled on, pushing the cart with all her might.

At dusk many years earlier, as sunset spread its colors across the sky, Wu Quan's wife was young and pretty. In those days nobody knew who she was going to marry. She and Wu Quan stood together on the bridge, as a wooden boat swung toward them and tree leaves and cabbage leaves floated on the water beneath the houses with their windows open. He happened to be crossing the bridge then with a bottle of cooking oil in his hand and he watched them from a distance, just as others did.

The wooden bridge had later been torn down and replaced by a concrete one. But now it was the wooden bridge that he saw.

2

The physics teacher's wife gazed at the wall of the old house that faced the earthquake shelter. Rain spilled down the wall, scattering in all directions like rays of light. A scene from long ago had taken on a new life. For the old wall was almost as green as grass, and as the rain spurted the wisps of light reminded her of a morning many years earlier when she sat at a table and saw how the windblown grass was bending away from her.

"*The sun came up.*" *The teacher read the text aloud.*

"*The sun came up.*" *The class repeated.*

"*And cast its rays everywhere.*"

"*And cast its rays everywhere.*"

The rays of sunrise grew on the tips of the grass, and the wisps of light were bending away from her. That morning long ago had come back to life, here by the old wall as the rain poured down.

The jubilant exodus of four days earlier had been just a passing glory. Once news came that there would be no earthquake, the PE instructor was the first to leave the shelters, soon followed by her husband and her, but they got no farther than the old wall. She could already see in the distance the cream-yellow door of home, only to have to turn around again.

Her mother, who lived behind another cream-yellow door, liked talking to her cat. "If you keep on being naughty, I am going to have to trim your fur."

She heard a moan nearby. Her husband's moans were as regular a fixture now as the patter of rain on the tarps.

When would the wind and rain end? When would sunshine come out of the textbook?

"And cast its rays everywhere."

"Illuminating the earth."

Where did that tearing sound come from?

Her husband sat by the entrance to the kitchen, tearing old pieces of cloth into strips.

"Making a mop," he said.

She turned and saw her husband tearing a shirt into pieces. Damp for so long, the shirt was well on its way toward disintegrating. He laid the pieces neatly on his leg.

She put her hand on his. "Don't do that," she said.

When he turned toward her, she saw a smug smile on his face.

He continued to tear up the shirt. She felt her hand drooping, and though she raised it once more it did not stay up.

"Don't do that," she repeated.

The smile spread across his face and he gazed at her defiantly as he tore another strip. He was trembling from the effort, and soon he stopped and his smile disappeared. Breathing heavily, he gripped the edge of the bed.

She looked away, and the old wall with the rain pouring down appeared once more.

"Where is Beijing?" she had asked.

Only one student raised his hand.

"Kang Wei."

Kang Wei stood up and pointed to his heart. "Beijing is here."

"Who else can answer?"

No other pupil raised a hand.

"Everyone now recite a lyric: 'I love Beijing's Tiananmen . . .'"

The bed shook as her husband rose to his feet. He knocked his head against the plastic tarp as he stepped out of the shelter and into the pouring rain. He stood there for a moment, his tattered shirt flapping in the wind and his rain-soaked back blocking her view of the old wall. Then he moved off and the wall reappeared.

That morning, rays of light had been slanting away.

"Liu Jing's dove," Father had said.

A white dove flew toward the rising sun, its feathers showing wisps of sunrise color.

The old wall was blocked once more, as a boy's figure appeared. He looked at her hesitantly. "I came to tell the physics teacher," he said, "the monitor has been normal throughout."

"Come in," she said.

The boy came in. His head knocked against the tarp but did not push it up. His coat was dripping.

"Take your coat off," she said.

He took it off, but remained standing.

"Have a seat."

The bed shook as he sat down on the end farthest away from her. Now another person was sitting on the bed. On days when late afternoon sunshine shone in through the window, it was warm there.

Had she already told him that the physics teacher would be back any minute?

Rain poured down the old wall.

A little flower called a lilac, its colors subdued, had quietly blossomed by the threshold of her house.

"It's a lilac," her sister had said.

That's how she learned that lilacs are not so very attractive.

"It's not as pretty as its name."

CHAPTER SIX

1

Late in the afternoon, Dawei came back alone. Li Ying's voice rang out forlornly in the rain. "You couldn't find him?"

"I went all over town." Dawei splashed his way toward her. And then there was no sound at all.

"I know where Xingxing is," Zhong Qimin said.

Wu Quan's wife lay in bed. Zhong Qimin sat in the chair by the window, his eyes fixed on her bulging midriff. In the murky light, it cast a shadow that rose and fell ever so slightly on the wall. Before long, a child would appear in the courtyard, toddling along with hesitant steps, one hand on the wall, and soon he would grow big, just as big as Xingxing.

Xingxing was not coming back.

"I know where he is," Zhong Qimin repeated.

When Wu Quan's wife returned from the crematorium, she did not go back to the shelter but went home instead, and in his mind Zhong Qimin went to see her there.

The flute music floated toward the rain outside. It was linked to a scene in which sunshine skimmed over water and brightly colored butterflies flitted about on a nearby lawn. But there was no child walking on the grass, for the child had not yet been born.

Zhong Qimin did not come in with Wu Quan's wife—he came into her house along with her swollen belly.

Now Wu Quan's wife was sitting up, her eyes as bright as water in the dark room.

Where the Grand Canal entered Hangzhou, fields stretched in all directions. Boys with sickles in their hands and baskets of grass on their backs—four of them, there should be—walked toward him, and the notes of the flute pulsed on the water.

Wu Quan's wife went on sitting there, while the rain beat down in a neat, precise tempo. As time passed, human clamor subsided and the rain was imbued with stillness, so that it seemed as stationary as the concrete utility poles outside. Rain had poured down the whole day in an unchanging rhythm and by its very monotony had become a form of quiet.

Wu Quan's wife stood up, her body sluggish as she turned. Was she planning to go upstairs? There would be a bed up there too. But instead she entered a small room—the kitchen, it had to be.

"Ah!"

A woman's screech, like that of a bird swooping down from a cliff.

"A snake!"

The scream hung in the air for a long time before it was carried off by the wind.

"A snake! There's a snake!" The cries became staccato.

There was the sound of someone dashing out of a shelter in panic and splashing frantically through the rain.

"There's a snake inside the shelter."

Nobody paid any attention.

"There's a snake."

Her voice became weak, and now she was talking to herself. Then she remembered to cry.

Why would nobody listen to her?

Her sobs circled around their heads, but her sobs were feeble and insubstantial, unable to knock a hole in the rain's stillness.

Zhong Qimin heard the clatter of a wok; she had probably started cooking. She needed to cook for two, although she was the only one to eat. The child inside her would soon come into the world, grow up rapidly, and then enter quietly and sit at his feet, listening to his flute.

As soon as the music sounded, it eclipsed her weeping.

When it's raining, flute music always has a link to sunshine. The sky should be blue; in the northlands, the earth and the sunshine are much the same color. He had once hiked there for a day, the notes of his flute resounding on the sunbaked earth. A boy appeared between some leafless trees, his skin at one moment as yellow as the earth and the next moment as yellow as the sunlight, or perhaps it was both at the same time. The boy began to tag along behind, his eyes as black as the ocean's deepest depths.

Wu Quan's wife was sitting on the bed once more and looking at him. Her eyes gleamed with a glance that looked almost like Xingxing's, but it wasn't her glance so much as the glance of the child-to-be. The still-unborn child had heard his flute and was looking at him with his mother's eyes.

Something fell down with a huge crash and there was the sound of someone struggling, his cries muffled.

It was Lin Gang's voice that finally emerged. "Wang Hongsheng, my shelter has collapsed!" He sounded rattled. "I thought it was an earthquake."

He cried again, "Wang Hongsheng, give me a hand, will you?"

No response.

"Wang Hongsheng!"

Wang Hongsheng's weary voice emerged from his shelter. "How about you come in here?"

Lin Gang stood in the rain. "I can't do that. How can three people fit in such a tight space?"

Wang Hongsheng said nothing.

"I'll do it myself." As Lin Gang yanked on the tarp, water cascaded down. Nobody went to help him.

Wu Quan's wife now stood up and went back into the kitchen; soon he heard the sound of a wok being lifted off the burner.

I ought to get back, he said to himself.

2

She felt beads of sweat crawling on her skin, glistening beads. What is it those broad-leaved trees are called? On bright mornings the leaves are covered in glistening drops of dew. Rays of the rising sun shine into the drops, creating rifts in them. The beads of sweat on her body had a similar sparkle, but no such rifts.

The pitter-patter repeated itself endlessly, but the moans had ceased a long time ago—was her husband never coming back? Later, it was that boy Bai Shu who arrived, and two people were sitting on the bed once more. This boy was always showing up—as soon as she thought of him he would appear. He would sit there quietly, with no moaning and no tearing of shirts, but there would still be two people sitting on the bed.

The rain on the old wall spattered everywhere as before. But now a gust of wind came and the leaves that hung over the earthquake shelters made a swaying sound that began to disrupt the uniform pitter-patter of raindrops. Inside the shelter the breeze brought a whiff of crisp, early morning coolness.

"Now we'll read the lesson," the Chinese teacher said. *"Chen Ling, read the fourth paragraph."*

She stood up. "The wind died, the rain stopped. . . ."

The old wall where the rain spattered was obscured by a body. It moved inside—it was her husband. Her husband's body pressed down on the bed. Bai Shu would be here very soon, but there were already two people on the bed. She felt her husband's eyes gleaming. One hand reached inside her clothes and made a beeline for her breasts; the other hand rested on her spine.

A boy very much like Bai Shu was sitting next to her desk.

"The wind died, the rain stopped. . . ."

Her husband's fingers were laden with familiar language, a language constantly repeated these past few years, calling her skin again and again.

Perhaps there had been such an afternoon when a youth came walking out of the sunshine, his dark hair waving in the breeze. Yes, he surely must have come out of the sunshine—that would be why she felt so warm.

The body next to hers stood up, and her own found itself controlled by a pair of hands. The hands helped her to her feet and led her toward the old wall where the rain danced. She felt rain on her face, along with a cooling breeze. Morning opened the window and she saw how the grass was dancing in the wind.

That pair of hands continued to guide her, a familiar voice was guiding her as her body and another's moved through the rain.

The rain had suddenly stopped, but the wind seemed all the fiercer. They were in a corridor, it appeared, with classrooms on right and left. Now they began to go upstairs, the other body leading her.

The folder holding her lecture notes fell onto the stairs and a heap of music scores scattered everywhere like snowflakes.

"Good students will pick them up for me."

Students were drifting like snowflakes, not far away.

Now they had reached the top of the stairs. Her body and the other one came into a room. There would be an organ next to the blackboard, and sunshine would slip through the cracks between the tree leaves and flow across the keys. Without her fingers the organ could not sing.

There seemed to be a clatter of desks being shifted, shrill like the shouts of the children on the playing field. The students on cleaning duty began to sweep the floor, their brooms knocking against one another, the dust flying like snowflakes, like song scores.

Again that familiar pair of hands was leading her, pressing

her, until her feet left the floor. Her body lay down and the hands began to talk to her clothes. The other body mounted hers, and one body called to another in conventional speech.

A sparrow had once flown in through the window, into the organ music and song. The children's glances followed the sparrow as it fluttered.

"Get it out of here."

The students rushed up, but it didn't look as though they meant to drive the bird away.

Something had entered her, she ought to be able to remember what. It was a sentence she'd often heard, a line one never got tired of using that had come in. Why was the body on top so agitated?

She understood now: the children were trying to capture the sparrow.

"Just leave it alone."

Later the sparrow flew out of the classroom all by itself.

3

When Dawei returned from town that afternoon, Li Ying's sobs, long suppressed, carried through the air once more.

Dawei had brought a child back with him. His shouts could be heard even as they were still in the alleyway. "Li Ying, Li Ying—I've found Xingxing!"

There was an outburst of weeping, and the sound of two pairs of feet tramping through water toward each other.

"Xingxing!" Li Ying wailed as she hugged the boy.

He struggled in her arms, his protests muffled.

"I found him next to the garbage dump." Dawei's voice was loud. "A typhoon is coming." Again he spoke loudly.

In the wind and rain only their voices could be heard. Nobody came out of the shelters to encroach on their relief.

"A typhoon is coming."

Why was Dawei so elated? Was it because of Xingxing's return, or because a typhoon was on its way?

Xingxing was back.

Wu Quan's wife sat on the bed looking at Zhong Qimin, who was raising his flute.

With his paper glasses Xingxing could see everything, and after his long outing he was back home again. Flute music filled the air.

Evening was approaching. *The fields stretched as far as the eye could see and the rays of the setting sun could not have been warmer. The path stretched across the fields in the same winding manner as a fish's passage through water, and somehow it had a way of returning to where it started: just so long as you kept walking straight, you would find yourself heading home.*

Li Ying's weeping trailed off. She was saying something to the boy, but the words were indistinct. Dawei shouted once more, "A typhoon is coming!"

Still they stood in the rain, but nobody came out to join them. They began to trudge toward the shelter.

Zhong Qimin waited until the splashing sounds had disappeared before raising his flute once more.

The image that came to mind was of a leaf that has just left the tree, its greenness unsullied by dust; as it neared the ground a gust of wind changed its fate. It landed on the stream, and water glinting with dappled sunlight clambered on top. It sank to the bottom, resting on earth, after all.

The sound of Dawei and the others was now replaced by wind and rain. Surely Xingxing would have heard his flute and would sneak out to linger by his feet. But the boy did not appear.

He began to recall where he was. Xingxing would not come here, for this window was not his. So he stood up and went outside, and through a sheet of rain he saw his own window in the distance. Xingxing was perhaps already sitting there. So that was where he went.

4

Much later, she became aware of how heavy her body felt as she returned to waking consciousness. Through the open window there came sounds of pelting rain. She turned and watched the trees trembling in the storm. Then she discovered that she was lying in the classroom, naked below the waist. Astonished, she rose hastily, dressed, and sat down in a chair.

When she tried to remember the scene prior to this, it seemed to have happened a long time ago. She could faintly hear the sound of a shirt being torn, and an image of her husband appeared jerkily in her mind and just as jerkily departed. Then it was Bai Shu who came into the picture, sitting quietly next to her.

Now she sat alone in the earthquake shelter. Whose body

was it that was blocking her view of the old wall? It had stretched out a hand to her, and so she lay down.

She stood up and walked toward the door. When she reached the staircase, the body that had led her upstairs came to mind once more, but she could not think whose it was.

At the bottom of the stairs she saw the earthquake shelter straight ahead of her, her husband sitting inside. She walked toward him.

When she sat down by his side, again she could picture herself half naked in the classroom, and she felt frightened. She put out an arm and clasped her husband's hand.

His head drooping, he showed no reaction whatsoever.

"Just now I—" Her voice sounded unfamiliar to her ears. "Please forgive me," she murmured.

Her husband's head was still bowed.

"Just now I—" she repeated. She thought a while, then shook her head. "I don't know."

Her husband tugged his hand away. "Too heavy," he said. His voice was weary.

Her hand slipped down to the edge of the bed. She said nothing more and began to gaze at the old wall where the rain was still coursing.

After what seemed like a long time, she faintly heard the loudspeaker at the school gate announcing that the typhoon was about to arrive.

The typhoon is coming, she told herself.

Tiles fell from the roof and shattered and a tree fell to the ground, exposing its mud-caked roots.

Her husband stood up now. Dragging his feet, he exited the shelter and disappeared in the rain. *After the typhoon the sun was bright. But the elm tree in front of the building had been blown over. She had asked her father, "Did the typhoon do that?"*

Her father was about to go out.

She noticed that the grass next to the tree was completely untouched and swayed in the breeze, in the sunshine. "Why wasn't the grass blown flat?"

5

Sayram Lake in spring is circled by snow-clad peaks, and a white bird darts over the water, its wings as dazzling as snow.

Zhong Qimin sat by his window, but Xingxing still did not appear. He finished playing the last tune that Xingxing had heard.

That boy is not Xingxing, he told himself. Then he stood up, went down the stairs, and came out into the rain. The raindrops were sparse now. He walked toward Wu Quan's house.

Wu Quan's wife was not sitting on the bed. As he stood by the door he saw that she had moved her possessions back into the shelter. The way she looked at him prompted him to join her, and he sat down next to her.

Just then the cries of an upset child emerged from Dawei's shelter. "I want to go home!" the boy cried. "I want to go home!"

"That's not Xingxing," he said.

6

Now again there were two people sitting on the bed.

Bai Shu took the red fruit from his pocket and offered them to the physics teacher's wife.

"What are they?"

Her voice had never sounded so close before, and it brought her scent to him. It was a damp, somewhat sour scent, but it was hers—and it came from the body under her clothes.

Her hand made contact with his, and she popped one of the wild fruit into her mouth. Her lips puckered, and a purple juice dripped quietly from the corner of her mouth. Then she looked at the other fruit nestled in his outstretched hand. She reached out and tipped them into her own palm.

He looked at her sideways. Her long neck, as pale as jade, bent forward slightly, beads of sweat on its surface. A little mole perched quietly on her neck—it had no reason not to be quiet. A few strands of black hair drifted down over her white skin. Her neck suddenly gave a wonderful little swivel: that was her head turning toward him.

Now there were two people on the bed. It had been that way for ages, it seemed. Her husband had gone out long ago. Later a body blocked her view of the old wall, when Bai Shu came and sat next to her. She began to remember, remember the body that led her into the classroom. Could it have been Bai Shu?

Now the view of the old wall was obscured again, this time

by two bodies, one behind the other. Someone asked, "Do you want a steamed bun?"

It was a man, she could see, with a woman behind him holding a basket.

"The buns are hot out of the steamer."

Bai Shu recognized the speaker as Wang Liqiang; his mother was with him. When she saw him, she tugged Wang Liqiang's arm and they hurried away.

The old wall in the pouring rain appeared once more. Many years ago, this same kind of rain had soaked the city where she used to live. Holding an umbrella over her head, she stood waiting for a trolleybus. Two youths huddled nearby, water dripping from their hair as though from the eaves of a house. Later one of them slipped in underneath her umbrella. "Is that all right?"

"Sure, that's fine."

The other youth, a very good-looking boy, went on standing in the rain, but threw her furtive glances.

"Is he your classmate?"

"Yes, he is."

"Hey, come and join us," she called to him. He turned and shook his head, blushing hotly.

"He's embarrassed."

The handsome youth went on standing in the rain.

There was another day in early summer, a day with radiant sunshine and no black clouds scudding across the sky, when he sat on a concrete block near the school gate, his legs dangling casually. Almost all the young teachers at the school were standing by the gate, a clear sign that the physics teacher's city wife would arrive that afternoon. Reports of her beauty had been circulating for some time already among Gu

Lin, Chen Gang, and Co. His legs waved ostentatiously as he watched the young teachers mopping sweat from their brows under the fierce sun. Next to him was a plane tree, and above his head its broad leaves were waving too.

Later the young teachers formed two lines at the entrance to the school, and he saw them break into applause, big grins on their faces, as the physics teacher and his wife approached. The physics teacher, though red with embarrassment, was brimming with pride; his wife kept her eyes lowered but chuckled gaily. She walked toward him in a black dress, a black dress that looked stunning in the bright sunshine.

ABOUT THE AUTHOR

Yu Hua is the author of five novels, six story collections, and four essay collections. His work has been translated into more than forty languages. He has received many awards, including the James Joyce Award, France's Prix Courrier International, and Italy's Premio Grinzane Cavour. Yu Hua lives in Beijing.

ABOUT THE TRANSLATOR

Allan H. Barr is the translator of Yu Hua's debut novel, *Cries in the Drizzle;* his essay collection *China in Ten Words;* his short story collection *Boy in the Twilight;* and his most recent novel, *The Seventh Day.* He teaches Chinese at Pomona College in California.

A NOTE ON THE TYPE

This book was set in Caledonia, a Linotype face designed by W. A. Dwiggins (1880–1956). It belongs to the family of printing types called "modern face" by printers—a term used to mark the change in style of the type letters that occurred around 1800. Caledonia borders on the general design of Scotch Roman but it is more freely drawn than that letter.

TYPESET BY SCRIBE,
PHILADELPHIA, PENNSYLVANIA

PRINTED AND BOUND BY BERRYVILLE GRAPHICS,
BERRYVILLE, VIRGINIA

DESIGNED BY IRIS WEINSTEIN